Mike Delaney had a successful career as a nurse before reaching out and going into residential treatment for his addictions in 1996. He has since become a renowned mental health/addictions therapist, having developed and been CEO and the Clinical Director of several new treatment facilities as well as having a successful private practice in Harley Street, London. He is currently the Clinical Director of Delamere Health, the UK's first, purpose built, Addiction and Behavioural Health Clinic in Cheshire and is regularly asked for his expertise in newspapers, magazines and on television.

I would like to dedicate this book to the many innocent young women across the UK, who were locked up for a lifetime in mental hospitals, when their only crime was falling pregnant out of wedlock. Many of them developed ongoing and serious mental health issues due to the trauma of being separated from family as well as having their child taken away.

In my long career as a nurse, I met and worked with many of them, older and wiser, but still traumatised by the loss of their children.

This book is for all of them, and to help people to understand the cruelty and judgement which was inflicted by society on these vulnerable young girls.

Mike Delaney

MABEL MURPHY

AUSTIN MACAULEY PUBLISHERS™
LONDON * CAMBRIDGE * NEW YORK * SHARJAH

A CIP catalogue record for this title is available from the British Library.

ISBN 9781528965125 (Paperback)
ISBN 9781528994873 (Hardback)
ISBN 9781398404953 (ePub e-book)

www.austinmacauley.com

First Published 2022
Austin Macauley Publishers Ltd®
1 Canada Square
Canary Wharf
London
E14 5AA

Thank you to my family for their love and support when I stopped doing anything else during the pandemic and just locked myself in my office every day to write.

A special thank you to my "theatrical" friends who continued to encourage me and believe in me when I wasn't sure what I was doing. Ann Mitchell, Libby McArthur, Kate Donnelly, Ann Hughes and a special shout out for Barbara Bryceland, who has supported all of my endeavours since my three-month isolation in Barbados in March 2020.

Table of Contents

1

It was a crisp evening in early 1930 and the daffodils were beginning to appear in the park in Leyton, East of London. Mabel was sitting on a bench with her friend Sarah, feeding some stale bread to the ducks, who seemed very hungry after such a long winter. "Do you think he'll come?" asked Sarah.

"Who?" said Mabel.

"You know!" said Sarah with a smirk. "Your boyfriend, Tom!"

"Well, I don't bleedin' know, do I?" said Mabel.

"When I saw him delivering on his bicycle today, he said he might see me here later, so who knows?" She folded up the empty brown paper from the bread and put it in the pocket of her dark woollen coat.

"You've really gone soft on him, ain't ya?" Sarah laughed. "You wanna kiss him on the lips, don't ya?" she called as she jumped from the bench to avoid Mabel's embarrassed slaps.

"Stop sayin' that, Sarah," she yelled smiling. "You know I'm not into all that stuff! I just think he's nice, that's all. Like me mate!" she said convincingly. "I ain't kissed anyone before, have you?" she asked.

"'Course not!" said Sarah. "I'm not grown up like you. Nobody ain't interested in me and I sure ain't interested in them!" she said firmly. "Anyway," continued Sarah. "You'll be 14 soon and you'll probably be working in Bearman's up in Leytonstone and it will only be a matter of time before you get married and have kids!"

"Bleedin' hell, Sarah! I ain't even kissed anyone and you've got me working in a shop and up the bleedin' duff! Gawds sake, I wanna do stuff, not just scrape by! Look at our house. It's tiny and cold with an outside loo. Me ma's sick all the time and my dad's working all hours. If it wasn't for Father Cullen, I don't know where we'd be!" she said, repeating her mum's words.

"He comes 'round our house as well," said Sarah. "He's a bit creepy but he brings food and sometimes clothes for the little 'uns. I always go into another room when he's in the house!"

"Yeah, I know what you mean," replied Mabel. "Sometimes he turns up when Mum's not well and I'm left with him, having to make him a cuppa tea and that. I always talk loudly and include me Mum, even if I know she's sleeping so I don't have to feel alone with him. Strange isn't?"

"Yeah," said Sarah knowingly. "It is bleedin' strange right enough…"

After a little while, when Tom doesn't appear, they stand up and start to stroll around the neatly kept little park, which has some nice flower beds, a few swings and a play area on one side and a small bandstand right in the middle. It was pretty quiet considering the main road with trolley-buses was just over the fence, not to mention the Central Line Underground which was above ground in this part of London.

Mabel called the park her quiet, thinking place. Not so much in the summer where it was full of families and noisy kids, but in the spring and summer evenings it was nice and was an escape from the stresses of the house.

"How's your mum?" Sarah asked.

"Yeah, she alright," answered Mabel. "Same as usual really," she added.

"What's actually wrong with her, Mabel?" asked Sarah. "Why does she stay in all the time?"

"Apparently it's all my fault," said Mabel. "The story goes she had terrible baby blues after she had me and never really got better. She lost a couple of babies after me as well. Every so often she has to go into that Claybury Asylum up in Chigwell for a little while to sort herself out. They have doctors and nurses who understand her and make her better. It's such a massive hospital it would take you a week to find anywhere. Giant corridors, like a maze!" said Mabel.

"Yeah, but what's wrong?" Sarah persisted.

"Well, I don't bleedin' know, do I? I'm not a bloomin' doctor!" said Mabel angrily, before calming down and quietly saying, "They call it Manic Depressed or somethin', and they give her pills every day, Lithium, I think. When she first goes into hospital, she sleeps a lot until they get the amount of tablets right, then she wakes up and starts to feel a bit better usually, but if that don't work, they put electric shocks in her head and make her have a fit!"

"No!" screamed Sarah. "Electric shocks? I ain't going near that place I can tell you! Your poor mum, no wonder she ain't well!"

As they headed back towards Leyton Green, they frequently stopped to natter to ladies they both knew who were out shopping or children who they knew from school, so it often took them some time to get back home. "They could both talk for England," they were always being told by adults.

1930 was just one of several bad years due to the great-depression. Mabel's dad, George, only kept his job at the docks by a whisker, as exports were right down and they laid-off hundreds of men. The agreement was that if he was kept on, he had to do much more work for the same pay, but George was a grafter and was just glad of the job. There wasn't any government support back then; if you didn't work, you didn't eat, as many of his former workmates knew. George would get up and cycle down to the East India Dock for a 6.00 am start and that would be him until at least 6.00 pm, depending on how many ships were in. It was hard, physical work, so when he finally got home, he usually just had a bite to eat and fell asleep in his chair, or sometimes while he was still sat at the table. Although his wife, Betty, didn't enjoy good mental health, she tried her best and, even though she didn't go out much, she tried to keep a good house and make sure there was always decent food to eat. Sometimes it might only be soup made from bones from Jackson the Butcher with a hunk of bread to dip, but it was filling and nutritious. Sometimes George would be lucky enough to get a free chicken down the docks and that would be a real treat when all the family would be over for Sunday Lunch.

Their house was a little two-up, two-down terrace, just off the Lea-Bridge Road, rented from a private landlord who didn't pay too much attention to the state of his houses. He would appear at the door every Friday evening to collect his 12 shillings rent but was never interested in doing any repairs.

"If you don't like it, Missus, there's plenty more who would love it!" he would say if they complained. It wasn't as bad as some of them, mind you; the outside toilet actually worked, and the roof didn't leak, but there were mice all over the house and cockroaches coming out of the wallpaper because of the flour and water paste they used to hang it with. There was a coal fire in the kitchen and sitting room, but they couldn't afford the coal to have both burning, so they spent a lot of time in the kitchen and lit the sitting room fire of a weekend, as sometimes they had a bit of company from old friends or family.

Betty's mum, Beryl, would pop in most days to check on her and to see the kids, she would always give a hand and do a bit of housework or washing that needed doing while she was in. She was quite a big woman and wore a 'wrap-around-pinnie' underneath her coat, saying "I'm always ready for action!" with a laugh. Similarly, her grey hair was usually wrapped tightly in a headscarf, a bit like a turban, but if she went down the Bakers Arms for a drink at the weekend, she would comb it out and set it in curlers.

Beryl was not afraid of hard work and fiercely protective of her family but was also very popular in the neighbourhood and nobody would dare say a word about her daughter Betty's illness, unless it was to inquire or offer some help. Everyone went to Beryl with their problems, no matter what they were, because she was a great listener and never told anyone else what had been said. She was no gossip. "A secret is a secret," she would say, and she truly meant it. She was also very funny, especially after a few drinks when she would get up and lead the singalong if she was out visiting friends or at the pub on a Saturday night. She knew all the old Maire Lloyd music hall numbers and got everyone to join in the choruses, pretending to conduct them as they sang along!

She had been widowed in the Great War so, like many other women in London, had been a single parent since 1917, working several different jobs to keep her family afloat, but they were all up and married now so, although she kept working, it was because she enjoyed working as opposed to being desperate for the money, although she had a very meagre life, ten cigarettes a day and the odd drink, but generally she was a home-bird, sitting in the evenings listening to the wireless with a cuppa and a bit of something home-made, like a scone or freshly baked bread with a bit of jam. After such a hard, and still very busy life, she enjoyed a bit of peace and quiet in the evenings when she could lose herself in the stories, plays or band music, just her and her wireless. Sometimes she would nod-off and miss the end of a story which drove her mad. "I sat there for a bleedin' hour and fell asleep the last few minutes! Gawd knows who the murderer was!" she would tell people the following day with a giggle, just to amuse them.

It was a couple of weeks after this when Betty took a bad spiral downwards into depression, a bit worse than usual. She didn't want to get out of bed at all and just kept saying "I'm so tired, darlin'" every time Mabel tried to motivate her into getting up.

"Mum, it's an absolutely beautiful day out there! Why don't we go for a walk over Wanstead Flats? that would make you feel better," she would suggest, but with no response. Mabel and her dad had just been saying the previous night that it may be time to call the doctors to see about getting her into Claybury Asylum, but that they would see how things went over the next few days. In the meantime, Mabel was trying to keep the house clean and make some mutton stew for her dad's dinner when he got home later. She was stirring the pan on top of the black-leaded range, feeling quite grown-up when a knock came to the front door. *Who can that be?* she thought to herself, *It's too early on a Friday for the rent and there's no money till Dad gets in anyway, so who the devil can it be?* She walked up the small hall and could see a large, dark silhouette, through the frosted glass panes of the door. "Oh, hello, Father Cullen," she said as she opened the door.

"Hello, Mabel, my child," he said. "I was just wondering how your mum was doing, I heard she wasn't too good."

"She's asleep, Father," said Mabel. "But I'll tell her you called when she wakes up." She was rather taken aback when he paid no attention at all to her words and barged past her into the hallway then proceeded to park himself down on a chair in the kitchen. She was sure she could smell whisky as she knew the smell from when her dad had the odd drink.

"Oh, something smells nice!" he said quietly.

"It's stew for my dad's dinner," Mabel said nervously, hoping he would go.

"He's a lucky man to have a beautiful and talented girl like you to cook for him," he said. "You'll soon have a husband of your own to look after now, won't you?" Mabel felt very uncomfortable but didn't know what to do for the best. She didn't want to upset him as he was an important person and if he told her parents she was rude, they would be very upset, so she stood quietly at the other side of the table.

"Are you not going to offer me some of that lovely stew?" he said.

"Sorry, Father, there's only enough for my dad when he gets in," she said timidly.

"Well, maybe you could make me a nice cup of tea and sit down with me for a while," he said. She was beginning to feel a little frightened as he was behaving strangely and hadn't even mentioned her mum, however she put the kettle over the fire and started to get the teapot ready. "Oh, never mind the tea, my girl, just come and sit here with me," he demanded as he patted the empty chair next to him.

"Do you ever feel a bit out of sorts Mabel? Like you just need someone to give you a cuddle and make everything better."

"Don't know Father," she said in a confused tone.

Mabel started to panic and didn't know what to do. He looked at her with determined eyes and continued to pat the empty chair, encouraging her to join him. "I'll just get your tea first, Father," she said, desperately wishing that her mum would wake up. His voice began to change into a quiet, but more menacing tone.

"Come here now," he said, "you don't want me to be upset with you now, do you?" Mabel slowly walked towards the priest, shaking but powerless to do anything. She sat next to him and he put his arm around her shoulder and pulled her in towards him. "That's a good girl," he said, stroking her face, "Father Cullen is feeling very lonely today, and God told me that you could help me with that feeling." Mabel was struck dumb as he slowly began to slide his other hand up her dress and stroke her inner thigh. "That's a good girl," he whispered, as he roughly forced his hand through the leg of her knickers and began to touch her intimately. Mabel was frozen, numb, and unable to move. Silent tears began to fall from her eyes as he grabbed her hand and placed it on his erect penis, which was now visible through his open black button-flies. "Oh yes," he whispered as he gently moved her limp hand up and down his genitals. "That's a good girl." Mabel was paralysed but, in her head, she was praying to God that it would stop. She focused on the noise of the stew bubbling as his fingers took away her innocence. Suddenly he became aggressive and pulled her over, lifted her dress and forced himself inside her, pulling her down on top of him and forcing her to silently suffer the pain of his thrusting. Then quickly, it was over, and after a few strange grunts, he lifted her gently off himself and sat her back down on the other chair. He buttoned himself back up and took her hand between his hands. "Oh, you've been such a good girl, Mabel, and God will be very happy that you've made me feel better," he said. "But we have to keep it between you, me and God, as people wouldn't understand. They would think you're a bad girl, but I know you're not and so does God." He patted her on the head and, without remorse or concern, said, "Tell your mother I called in, but she was asleep." And he walked proudly out of the house.

Mabel sat in shock and silence, unaware of the full impact of what had just happened. She stared into space, unable to comprehend how her body felt, still listening to the sound of the stew bubbling. She stood up and slowly walked to the fireplace, pulled the pan and kettle off the heat, and wondered what to do. She looked down at her dishevelled clothes and noticed blood on her dress and down her legs. She quickly Poured the hot water from the large kettle into a basin and got some soap and a cloth to clean herself before her mum woke up or her dad got in. She couldn't stop crying, completely traumatised by events and still unable to make sense of it.

Time passed quickly without her even noticing. She suddenly realised it was dark and she had been sitting staring into space for hours. She put the stew back on the fire as her dad would be home soon and she knocked on the bedroom door and said, "Mum, you hungry? You fancy a bit of stew?"

"No thanks, love," said her mum. "How long have I been sleeping darling? Did I hear Father Cullen?" Mabel felt her body begin to shake and for a minute she thought she was going to be sick.

"Yeah, he popped in, Mum," she said before she walked back into the kitchen and sat down until she stopped shaking.

The next few days were a bit of a blur for Mabel as she continued to struggle with the gravity of her attack and what she could do about it. Father Cullen hadn't called-in whilst she was there which was a blessed relief, but she felt anxious and fearful a lot of the time which was alien to her. She was normally confident and self-assured so found these new body sensations frightening, plus she was also very concerned about what God might think as she knew what she had done was bad and she was beginning to believe that it was all her fault and that she must have somehow provoked the assault.

2

Mabel bumped into Tom a few days later, on her way home from the shops and forced a smile when she saw him.

"Where 'ave you been hiding then?" he asked with a beaming smile as he sat astride his bicycle.

"Oh, you know," said Mabel. "Been a bit busy."

"You fancy going out for a walk later," said Tom. "We could stop and get an ice-cream."

Mabel wanted so much to say yes, but she felt so unworthy of his attention. "Sorry, not today, Tom, got to see to Mum," she said awkwardly, as she put her head down and carried on walking. About a week later, she came out of the greengrocers on Leyton High Rd with some fresh veg and he was standing waiting for her.

"You avoiding me, Mabel Murphy?" he asked assertively. "I ain't seen more than a glimpse of you for weeks and I don't know what I've done to upset you."

Mabel suddenly felt very emotional and could feel the tears welling-up behind her eyes. "Don't, Tom, I've just been busy," she replied, trying to hide the tears which were slowly running down her cheeks.

"What's wrong, Mabel?" he said, as he tried to put his arm around her shoulder. "I don't like to see you upset like this, who's done this to you?"

"Oh, Tom, don't be nice to me, you'll make me worse," she said as she began to sob. Tom put both arms around her and held her tight and she felt like she could stay there forever, quietly sobbing but feeling protected.

People were starting to stare so Tom said, "Let's go and get a cup of tea, Mabel, eh?" She wiped her eyes and nodded her head as he put his arm around her shoulder and led her to the little tea-room on the next corner. They sat at an empty table and the waitress walked over to them, looking very stern in her black uniform with white apron and hat.

"What can I get you?" she asked politely.

"Erm, a pot of tea for two please," said Tom.

"Anything to eat?" enquired the waitress.

"No, just tea for me please," said Mabel.

"Yes, just the tea then, thanks," added Tom.

"So, what's going on, Mabel? Is it your mum again?" enquired Tom.

"I wish that was all it was, Tom, but I just can't talk about it yet. I'll tell you when I'm ready so please don't keep mithering me about it yeah."

"Alright, love, I'm here when you're ready to talk to me, so remember that," he said reassuringly. The waitress arrived with the tray of teapots and dishes, so they just pretended that everything was OK and started to gossip about everything that was happening around the area.

As he walked her home and was leaving her at the door, she smiled at him and said, "Thanks for today, Tom, I was feeling really awful when I met you but I'm a lot better now. You've been a real tonic."

"No problem, madam!" he said as he doffed his flat cap with a smile and gently kissed her cheek before she ran into the house giggling.

"Who's that you were jawin' with out there, young lady?" said her mum, who was sitting at the kitchen table.

"Oh, it's only me mate, Tom, Mum. He just walked me back from the shops," said Mabel as she started unpacking the veg from the greengrocers.

"About time you were back, Mabel, can you be a darlin' and sort that veg for the soup? Your dad will be in soon," said her mum. "I've swept the floors and cleaned out the fire but I'm just feeling exhausted now."

"Don't worry, Mum, I'm back now. You can have a rest," said Mabel as she gave her mum a huge cuddle.

"What would I do without you, Mabel Murphy? You're a Godsend," said her mum with a tear in her eye and a grateful smile on her face.

As the weeks passed, Mabel managed to avoid Father Cullen who only seemed to 'pop-in' when he knew she was out, which gave her some relief from the anxiety, but she still started to shake when she heard his name and couldn't contain her emotions. Her dad even asked if she was OK one evening when her mum mentioned that Father Cullen had knocked that day and Mabel stood up from the table without finishing her meal and said, "I'm going to go and see Sarah."

"Hold on a minute, Mabel, what's going on girl? You're leaving good food on your plate and rushing off somewhere? Sit down and tell me what the devil is going on young lady!"

"Oh, Dad!" she protested. "It's nothing, I'm just not hungry."

He looked at her with the most serious face he could muster, as he loved her dearly and knew how wonderful she was at looking after her mum, but sternly said, "Listen to me, Mabel, I don't want to shout, and I don't want to repeat myself either, so listen good! There's a depression going on all around the world, which means there's no work and no money so, some folk, not a million miles from here I might add, have got no bleedin' food! It's selfish and ungrateful to waste good food, when some of our neighbours have got nothing!"

Mabel felt ashamed and sat back down, knowing that it was nothing to do with anything like selfishness, but more like when she hears the priest's name, she fills with a strange energy and she can't seem to sit still. "Sorry, Dad," she said quietly. "I'll finish my food and do the dishes. I don't need to see Sarah tonight."

As it transpired, they both thought that Betty was improving without hospitalisation, however she went missing one day and was brought home by the local 'Bobby' who found her wandering down Gainsborough Rd in Leytonstone, wearing only her nightdress. She was quite distressed and was lashing out if anyone came near her, so the policeman put his heavy coat around her and brought her home. Despite the best efforts of George and Mabel, she had to be taken to Claybury as, just like on a previous occasion, she thought that someone was poisoning her food, so wouldn't eat or drink and, apart from the constant agitation and exhaustion, she was losing weight fast. Two attendants came from the asylum in a big black car, came into the house and held her down whilst they gave her an injection in the bottom, and then put her in a straight-jacket as she was still trying to scratch and bite them. The neighbours were all out watching as she was carried out, screaming, and put into the back seat with one of the attendants.

George looked around the small street and shouted, "Show's over! You can all go back indoors now!" which caused most of them to feel uncomfortable and look at the ground as they pretended to sweep their steps or walked back in their front doors.

A few neighbours whom he knew well, stayed and approached him. "She'll be alright now, George, they'll take care of her and she'll be home as right as rain," said Kitty who lived a few doors down.

"I know, Kitty, but it doesn't get any easier," he said as he headed through his own door.

"You wanna cup of tea, Dad?" asked Mabel as she could see how upset he was.

"Yeah, go on, my girl, let's have five minutes and put a plan together over a cup of tea," he said, knowing that Mabel would have to do most of the work in whatever plan they came up with to manage Betty's absence.

The following weekend they borrowed a bicycle for Mabel from a neighbour and both cycled up to Chigwell to visit Betty. They got off at the imposing entrance gates, high, black, ornate, wrought iron gates attached to a wall on each side and, to the left as they entered, there was a small gate-lodge house. As they walked up the steep entrance road, they were filled with dread about what they might find and what state Betty would be in.

The asylum was massive, around 260 acres and had space for about 2,000 patients (called lunatics at the time). The male and female sides each contained three two-storey ward blocks for sick and recent cases. These blocks held around 650 patients divided among 12 wards. The blocks were connected by single storey corridors which also connected to the administration building, the chapel and the recreation hall.

They were very large corridors so were heated and ventilated so that they could be used for exercise in bad weather. Visiting took place in a sectioned off part of a corridor on each side. It was a very imposing and frightening construction, and the sounds of hysterical screaming could frequently be heard piercing the silence as you approached the main buildings.

George and Mabel parked their cycles and walked into the large, highly polished corridor, which lead to the female block. "Is it the same place as last time, Dad?" asked Mabel.

"I expect so," replied George. "Nothing much ever changes in this place." As they approached the screened-off area, they could see female nurses in blue uniform with white aprons and male 'attendants' in white coats over grey suits controlling the entry points to the visiting areas.

"Who are you here to see?" asked the stern-looking nurse.

"Betty Murphy," said George quietly. She ran her finger down the list of patients who had been approved visits until she saw the name.

"That's lovely, in you go, she's over there sat at a table," said the nurse pointing to the other end of the space.

"There she is, Dad!" said Mabel, rushing over to where her mum was sat. "Hello, Mum," she said as she kissed her on the cheek. Betty moved her head towards Mabel, as if in slow motion, and looked at her blankly. "It's me, Mum, Mabel!" she said, trying to evoke recognition or response.

"Mabel," she said, very slowly with a hint of a smile.

"Hello, my darlin'!" said George enthusiastically as he planted a kiss on her lips. "How are you doing?"

"George," she said, as if in a fog, "what's going on?"

"Oh, love," said George. "You ain't been too well, so the doctors felt you needed to come in for some convalescence."

"Oh," she slowly replied. "Sorry, I'm a bit sleepy and confused today. You takin' me home then?"

"Not yet, love," said George. "You're not quite there yet, another week or two should hopefully do it."

An attendant came to the table pushing a heavy metal trolley containing a huge two-handled teapot with lots of white cups and saucers. "Cuppa tea, anyone?" said the attendant.

"Yes, we'll all have one please," said George. The attendant put out the cups and saucers and filled them with milky tea from the large pot.

"No sugar, I'm afraid," said the attendant as he wheeled the trolley to the next table. Betty sipped her tea and began to look a little brighter.

"How's your ward, Mum?" asked Mabel.

"Noisy," said her mum. "I'm glad to get my tablets cos there's a woman who screams all day and night. No blessed relief at all."

"Why does she scream, Mum?" asked Mabel.

"Gawd knows, love," said Betty. "I think I heard a nurse say she lost a baby, but I'm not sure with these bleedin' tablets. Maybe I dreamt it." She took another sip of tea and said to George, "You takin me home then?"

"Oh darlin', you already asked me that. I wish I was, but not yet."

"When?" she replied.

"Soon," said George as he stroked her hand.

Every so often another patient would approach the table looking for food or cigarette ends out of the ashtray. She had a scary look in her eyes and would rock back and forth on her feet while she surveyed the table for leftovers. She suddenly grabbed the cup which Mabel was drinking out of and shouted, "You fuckin' done?" as she spun on her feet and drained the tea, leaves and all, before throwing the cup back on the table and bounding off to raid another table.

"Oi! Helen!" called an attendant. "If I see you do that again, you go back to the ward and no visit!"

"Fuck off!" screamed Helen. "Don't want no fucking visit, I want me tea!" Very quickly another two attendants appeared, and she was wrestled to the floor roughly and carried through the crowd of visitors back to the ward.

Betty looked across the room and saw a young girl sitting at a table with her dad, crying her eyes out. "Aw look, Dad, I think that must be her mum who was swearing just now," said Mabel, full of empathy and compassion.

"We have to count our blessings my darlin'," said George as he held Betty's hand tenderly and gave her a loving smile.

"Yeah, you're right, Dad," said Mabel, holding her mum's other hand.

After about half an hour, Betty started to fall asleep and a nurse appeared and abruptly said, "I better take her back to the ward now, say your goodbyes and go back the way you came in." They both stood up and kissed Betty as the nurse took her by the arm and led her out of the visiting area. George pretended to cough and discreetly wiped a tear from his eye, but Mabel couldn't hold it and went into floods of tears.

“Oh Dad!” she cried. “I hate leaving her in this place!”

“I know, darlin’,” said George as he rubbed her back. “Not long now…” And they headed back down the huge corridor to the main entrance.

3

Three weeks later and Betty was back home, looking very well and feeling much better too. Mabel had spent a long time making sure the house was spotless and she had also been out shopping and cooked a special dinner with a boiled ham her dad had managed to get from Jimmy Williams down the docks. As they all sat at the table tucking into the welcome home feast, Betty looked at Mabel and said, “You alright, darlin’? You look a bit peaky.”

“I’m just happy to have you home, Mum,” said Mabel.

“I don’t like it when you’re not here.”

“Well, I’m home now, love, so you can rest for a bit, you look so tired,” said her mum worriedly. “You look as if you’re filling-out as well love. A proper little woman.”

“Yeah, Mum, I’m putting on some weight, I can feel my dresses getting a bit tighter, so I’ll have to watch what I’m eating,” said Mabel embarrassingly.

“Go away,” said George. “There’s nothing of you girl!”

Just then, there was a knock at the door. “Who the bleedin’ hell can that be?” said George.

“I’ll get it, Dad, it might be Sarah, she said she might call around,” said Mabel. She rushed out of the kitchen and opened the front door to be greeted by the Priest. She stopped dead in her tracks, her expression changed, she began to shake, and she didn't know what to say.

"Who is it?" called George from the kitchen, but Mabel couldn't speak.

"It's me! Father Cullen! I heard that your lovely wife was back home!" he called as he squeezed past Mabel and patted her head.

"Oh, do come in, Father!" said George. "Have you eaten yet? Would you like to join us for a bite?"

"Thank you, but no, George, I'm on my way to Mrs Fulton, she's very poorly indeed so I just wanted to say welcome home to Betty, and I hope you're feeling better?"

"Thank you, Father Cullen, you're such a good man. I'm feeling much better thanks and glad to be home," said Betty.

"I won't keep you then, I'd better be off. I'll call in one day and see you, Betty!" he said as he headed back out to the hallway.

"See, Father Cullen, to the door, Mabel," said George. Mabel walked silently behind the priest as he opened the front door. He stepped out and turned to look at her, with a nasty glint in his eye.

"I'll be seeing you very soon, Mabel Murphy," he said as he slowly walked away from the house.

Betty remained fairly stable emotionally after her stay in Claybury, even managing out a few times to go to the shops with Mabel or just out for a stroll in the early evenings, sometimes as far as Walthamstow. On one occasion, they were sitting in the park chatting when Mabel suddenly got a piercing pain in her lower abdomen, so much so, that she screamed out and bent-over, holding her stomach tight.

"Whatever's the matter, Mabel?" cried her mum as she tried to help but didn't know what to do.

"Oh, Mum!" screamed Mabel. "My stomach!" Betty was panicked but took control of the situation, sat her down on a bench and tried to calm her down.

"Listen, love," she said. "Dr Raglan is just around the corner, can you make it to there?"

"Oh, please, Mum, let's go! I can't bear this!" cried Mabel as her mum helped her up and supported her to walk the short distance.

As they entered the doctor's office, they were met by a stern looking lady at a desk who took one look at Mabel and said, "What's the problem?"

"We don't know!" shouted Betty. "One minute she was OK and the next she was writhing in agony!"

"It's five shillings to see the doctor and then it's extra for any medicines or treatments," said the secretary lady.

"Yes, whatever you say!" said Betty impatiently. "Can we see him? Please!"

The lady knocked on the doctor's heavy wooden door and went inside, returning very quickly and showing them both in. The doctor was a heavy-set man and sat behind a huge mahogany desk, topped in green leather. The floors right through from the waiting room were also highly polished dark green linoleum and there was a strong smell of rubbing alcohol and disinfectant in the air. "Have a seat," he said to Betty whom he recognised from a visit to the house some years ago. "And you come through here with me," he said gently to Mabel as he pulled the screens around a dark green leather examination bed.

"You'll be alright now, darlin'," said Betty as she felt her strength begin to fade and the familiar anxiety and fear re-enter her body. She couldn't hear what they were saying but was thinking that Mabel must have eaten something that was off, but she had been cooking and knew that there was nothing bad at home. She then thought it may be appendicitis, as she had heard a few people talk about that. She sat quietly, slightly rocking to soothe her anxiety when the screens were moved back, and Mabel was straightening her clothing. Betty looked at Mabel for some information as she no longer seemed to be in any pain, but Mabel shrugged her shoulders as if to say she didn't know what was going on.

Come and sit down here my girl, said Dr Raglan as he pointed to the empty chair beside her mum. "Doctor, what's going on please?" said Betty. "I'm worried sick as I don't think she's been right for weeks now."

"Well, Mrs Murphy," said the doctor in an authoritarian tone. "There's no easy way to say this, so I will just say it. Your 14-year-old daughter is with child!" Betty thought that her heart was going to burst right out of her chest.

"There must be a mistake doctor! My Mabel's a good girl and couldn't be expecting!"

"There's no question, Mrs Murphy, I would estimate she's about four or five months," said the doctor knowingly. "No question at all, and the pain she was having was probably just a bit of movement and the baby pressing on some nerves."

Betty looked at Mabel in shock and disgust. "Mabel? Tell me? What's going on? Who have you been messing about with? Is it that Tom you keep talking about? Oh my God, your Father! What the hell am I going to do?"

Mabel broke down into heavy sobbing with very little comprehension about what they were saying. "I ain't done nothing, Mum! I promise!" She cried but her mum was on high anxiety alert and couldn't cope with the information she was being given.

"How the hell can she be so far gone, doctor? There's nothing of her!"

"That's why you haven't noticed," he said, "because she's a slight girl but if you put your hands on her stomach you will clearly see that it isn't fatty, its firm and distended."

"What do I do, doctor?" pleaded Betty with tears running down her face. "This can't be happening!"

Doctor Raglan sat up straight behind his desk and said, "I can put you in touch with a local doctor who will get her into a home for young mother's, they're out of the way, not local, so no one will know, and once she's had the baby adopted, you can decide what's best for her."

"She's only a baby herself," said Betty, sobbing uncontrollably, looking at Mabel who was finally beginning to understand that she had a baby growing inside her.

"Mum," she said through her sobs. "I'm sorry. I don't know what's happened." And she covered her face with her hands and cried like a baby.

Doctor Raglan passed a written note in an envelope giving details of the doctor they needed to see and said, "I'm very sorry, Mrs Murphy. You have enough to deal with, without all of this. My secretary will sort out your bill for today."

They walked in silence most of the way home, with tears flowing, stunned and traumatised by the revelations. As they got close to the house, Betty grabbed Mabel by the arm and said, very quietly but very seriously, "Don't you breathe a word of this to a living soul. Do you hear me? I still don't know what I'm gonna say to your dad, so you don't say a word, got it? Now straight up to bed when we get in or your dad will know something is wrong!"

"Yes, Mum," said Mabel through her blinding tears. "I'll bring you some food when it's done and, in the meantime, get your dresses ready, cos I'll have to let them out a bit. I don't wany anyone finding out about this." Mabel went straight to her bed and lay down, still crying but trying to work out exactly what was going on. She didn't know very much about sex at all so, deep down, she knew it was Father Cullen's doing on that awful day. She was thinking about what was best and what she could do about the mess she was in. If she told her parents about Father Cullen, just like he said, they wouldn't believe her, so she would be a 'bad girl' for having a baby and a terrible liar into the bargain for blaming a holy priest. The whole situation was going around and around in her head and it was getting more confusing and frightening, rather than easier. After a little while, her mum came into the room with a plate of food.

"I've told your dad you're not feeling well and will be staying in bed till tomorrow. If you need the toilet, use the chamber pot 'cos your face is all red with crying and your dad will know in an instant something is wrong."

"Alright, Mum," she replied as she again started to cry. "What am I going to do, Mum? Oh Mum, I'm so sorry." She sobbed.

"I need time to think, Mabel, stop crying and sort yourself out. I'll talk to you in the morning," said her mum as she closed the door behind her.

Mabel was awake most of the night, worrying and puzzling about what had happened. She imagined having a baby in the pram and walking down the road but then thought about the shame and judgement which would undoubtedly be hurled at her. Maybe it's best to go to the home, she thought, at least until everything settled. She heard the front door close as her dad left for work and went running downstairs. Her mum was sitting at the table with a half empty cup of tea and a cigarette. She looked up at Mabel and slowly looked away without acknowledging her.

"Morning, Mum," said Mabel desperately.

"Don't you 'morning Mum' me, my girl," said Betty angrily, but quietly, in case anyone could hear her. "We've got some talking to do and some decisions to make before there's ever a good morning in this house again," she said with a scowl. Mabel began to cry again and pleaded with her mum to believe that she was a good girl and hadn't been messing about with boys.

"I ain't even kissed Tom proper, Mum," she said which made Batty erupt and bang the table with her fist.

"Well how the bleedin' hell are we in this predicament then, Mabel? Tell me that!" she roared.

"I don't know, Mum! I swear I don't!" cried Mabel, but Betty was not serving sympathy today and stood up from the table.

"You best get washed and dressed cos we've got to go out and see this doctor," she said as she held up the envelope from the day before. "Maybe he can help us!"

"It was Father Cullen!" screamed Mabel and she began to wretch and shake violently at her disclosure.

"You what?" said Betty angrily. "What did you just say to me?" Mabel couldn't speak, she lost control of her body and couldn't make it do anything she wanted. Betty was so enraged that, for the first time ever, she slapped Mabel hard across the face. "Don't even speak to me, girl!" she said, as Mabel collapsed in a weeping mess on the floor.

She saw her mum go to the shelf where she kept her medicines and take some of her Lithium tablets. "You're gonna be the death of me, Mabel Murphy!" she said as she threw them into her mouth and washed them down with the last of her tea. "Get dressed. We have someone to see," she said calmly and walked out of the room. Mabel felt herself begin to settle down and stop shaking, then the tears returned with a vengeance. At that moment, she thought about the priest, and how right he was that nobody would understand or believe her, and she began to fill with anger and hatred towards him.

They arrived in the office of Dr George Mitchell in Farringdon and explained to the small, elderly man what the situation was. "Oh dear," he said. "Oh dear, dear, dear," he repeated as he shook his head. "This is a terrible situation for your family," he said to Betty, as if Mabel wasn't present. "A terrible situation." Mabel tried to speak but he very quickly said, "And I'll hear nothing from you, young lady! You are the problem here!"

Mabel was shocked as no one ever spoke to her like this before. She looked at her mum in the hope that she would defend her, but Betty was still angry and full of shame, so looked at her in the same way that the doctor did. He cleared his throat and looked at Betty. "I know a mother and baby home, run by the Church near Maidstone in Kent. You will have to pay for her to be there and she will have to work for her keep. Once the baby has been born, if it's fit and healthy, the nuns will find good adoptive parents who really need and deserve a child, and it will be given an opportunity to have a life, far better than you could ever provide," he said firmly and without an opportunity for discussion.

Betty was overwhelmed and upset by the whole situation and told herself that she was simply trying to do what was best. She knew that she, herself, had mental problems and probably wouldn't be able to manage any of the scandal, let alone manage a baby but the thought of telling George filled her with terror. He may blame her, and she couldn't cope with even the possibility of that. She feared that she would most likely have a break-down and would be forced back into Claybury, maybe this time never getting out. "Thank you, doctor, I will talk to my husband tonight, but I would like to take the offer of the mother and baby home. At least, she'll be safe with the nuns, there'll be no mischief there," she said.

"I'll make all the arrangements Mrs Murphy, if you bring her back here on Friday morning and leave her with me, I'll get her taken down to Kent," he said as he handed her a printed sheet with information about fees to be paid and a long list of rules for girls and their families.

Mabel heard her father scream from downstairs when her Mum gave him the news. She heard Betty crying and shouting, "No, George!" as she felt his heavy boots stomp up the wooden staircase. Her bedroom door crashed open and her father stood in the doorway with an expression she had never seen before.

"Tell me now, exactly what happened, and don't even think about blaming Father Cullen, young lady!" He snarled through gritted teeth. "What the fuck has happened to you?" Mabel was terrified and had never heard her dad swear, except if he was joking when he had a drink. Again, she took a breath to try to defend or explain herself, but no words would come out. Her whole body began to shake, and she filled with terror and panic. She could see vivid images of Father Cullen in her mind and could smell his sweat and the whisky on his breath.

"Have you got nothing to say, Mabel Murphy?" he screamed, but she couldn't. Her legs buckled and she fell to the floor, unable to support herself. She thought she was going to die in that moment as she couldn't breathe or make her body get back up. She sobbed quietly as her dad stormed out of the front door, slamming it behind him.

"See what you've done, Mabel!" yelled Betty. "This is all your fault!"

Not very long after her dad stormed out, Mabel's gran, Beryl, arrived, unannounced, and walked into the kitchen where both mother and daughter were sitting in silence as Betty unpicked some of the seams to let out Mabel's dresses. "Alright! I just briefly saw George heading into The Drum and when I said hello, he damned near took me head off! What's going on in this house? I'm not one to pry, but I've seldom seen George raise an eyebrow never mind raise his voice! Come on. Out with it!" she demanded as she slipped her coat off and threw it over the back of a chair. Betty looked up from the table at her mum, then looked across the table at her daughter. "We've got a bit of a problem, Mum," said Betty. "Mabel's brought shame to the door by getting herself into trouble." Beryl's face fell as she knew exactly what that phrase meant, she had seen it happen many times, but not to a 14-year-old. "Jesus, Mary and Joseph," she said as she made the sign of the cross on her chest. She was visibly shaken and pulled out a chair to sit down at the table.

Mabel had already started crying when Betty joined her and said, "Oh, Mum, what a bloody mess we're in."

"Right!" said Beryl. "Crying never solved nothing, what are you going to do?"

"I'm just letting these dresses out as the doctor has got her into a mother and baby home down Maidstone way, so she goes Friday Morning. Best that way, before she really starts showing," said Betty.

"Is it a decent place?" asked Beryl. "Yeah, it's the nuns who run it so it'll be strict but fair I imagine," said Betty.

"And what have you got to say for yourself young lady?" she asked Mabel accusingly. "I'm sorry, Gran," said Mabel, breaking down again.

"How far gone?" Beryl asked.

"Doctor thinks four or five months," said Betty.

"Come 'ere, darlin'," said Beryl lovingly, as she summoned Mabel over to her, "come to Gran." Mabel let out a wounded roar and ran towards Beryl, getting squeezed tightly by her strong, safe arms. "You'll be alright my girl, you'll be alright," she said as she comforted her granddaughter, then she leaned across and squeezed Betty's hand. "And you're gonna have to be very strong, Betty," she said. "But I'm here to help you both. Remember that."

George got back to the house late and very drunk. Betty was sitting up waiting when he arrived. "You alright, love?" she asked nervously as he staggered into the kitchen.

"I'm drunk, love, so who knows how I fucking feel!" he snapped as he dropped down onto a kitchen chair. "Have you sorted everything?" he asked.

"Yes, love, I borrowed a little case from my mum so I've packed her stuff, which isn't much mind you, but she shouldn't be away too long, eh love?" she said.

George wiped tears from his eyes and said, "I want to know how this happened. Is it that little brat Tom?" he asked.

"I don't know, love," she replied, "every time I ask her about anything, she just falls to pieces and won't tell me, but he's the only one she's ever spoken about these last few months."

"He'll rue the day he was ever fucking born if I get my hands on him!" he slurred. "Mark my fucking words!"

4

It was Friday morning and George left early, as usual, for work, still not having spoken to Mabel since he was told the news, as he still couldn't look at her without flying into a rage. Mabel's small suitcase was sitting in the hallway by the front door ready to pick up and both her and Betty were sitting at the kitchen table having a cup of tea before they left.

"Mum, I will be home soon, won't I?" asked Mabel.

"Please, God," she replied. "I'm gonna say you're staying with my Aunt Jen in Southend if anyone asks, that way, no one will wonder where you've gone and I can take the blame, saying you were very tired with looking after me."

"Thanks, Mum," said Mabel, relieved that she was getting any conversation at all from her mum. "Will you come and see me?" she asked.

"Don't think it's allowed 'til after it's all over and done with," came the terse response. "We'll see." They arrived at Dr Mitchell's office around 11.00 am and after a flustered and awkward conversation in the waiting room, Betty was ushered back out into the Farringdon streets to make her way back home to Leyton. She felt bewildered and lost as she looked around and wondered how on earth things had come to this.

Meanwhile, inside the office, Mabel was being spoken to like a schoolchild by the doctor.

"You will do as your asked by the Sisters. You will not answer back. You will not attempt to leave the home, at any time, and will not speak to anyone who visits or works in the home…" She began to lose concentration and to dream about the day she would be coming home. "That will keep me going. The day I come back here," she said to herself as Dr Mitchell continued to bombard her with rules.

After sitting for some time, the main door opened and two sharp-featured nuns walked in, looking her up and down as they went to the desk and chatted to the lady. Mabel could only hear whispers as they both turned to look at her and turned away again. Dr Mitchell then re-entered from his office and said, "Good morning, Sisters, I trust you had a safe journey?"

"It was very good, thank you," said one of them, "our driver is waiting right outside so we cannot be too long."

"No problem at all," said Dr Mitchell, "she's waiting for you right there and here is an envelope from her mother with payment for you."

"Thank you so much, doctor," said the same nun as she turned to Mabel and said, "Up on your feet girl and pick up that case. I'm Sister Augusta and this is Sister Frances. You don't speak unless spoken to, is that understood?"

"Yes, Sister," replied Mabel. They escorted her out of the office and into the back seat of a large black car where one of them sat on each side of her.

"Home please, Mr Jenkins," said Sister Augusta. "And don't spare the horses," said Mr Jenkins with a smile. "Indeed," said Sister Augusta, and those were the only words which were spoken for the whole journey. As they drove through some very grand gates, she could see a beautiful old building in the distance, surrounded by pristine, manicured gardens. There were lots of windows and a pointed tower at each corner with a cross sticking out of the top. The main door was black with a huge gold knocker and it was housed in an entrance porch with stone pillars on either side. As they approached the door it was opened from the inside and a nun slowly bowed her head as they walked past. Inside the main hall was very ornate, with highly polished wood, some stained-glass windows and large statues of The Virgin Mary, Jesus, and some other saints whom Mabel didn't know.

"Right, girl!" said Sister Augusta. "You won't be needing that case so leave it here. We have uniforms here!"

"But, Sister," she tried to say as she also had some personal items like her mum's rosary beads and a little prayer book. "What did I say to you about speaking when not being spoken to?"

"Sorry, Sister." She whispered. "I just wanted my personal things."

Sister Augusta stood tall and took a deep breath. "There are no personal things here, girl! You lost the right to have personal things when you did the devils work and indulged in carnal sin with men! We are now going to work the devil out of you and make you sorry you ever became a whore!" Mabel was terrified and began to cry. She had heard people talking about whores, but she thought that they were old, drunken women who were loud and bawdy. *How could the Nuns think she was like that when she was only a young girl?* she thought.

Sister Augusta snapped her fingers at the nun who opened the door and pointed at Mabel. "Take her up to the large dormitory in the attic and get her out of those clothes. You're not anything special anymore, girl. You are nothing!" Mabel was grabbed by the nun and pulled up several flights of stairs. As each new floor appeared, it looked more sparse and less ornate than the last. Eventually there was a winding wooden staircase which led to the attic room. As Mabel took the final steps, there emerged a very dark roof-space, with about five beds squeezed on each side of the room. There were no possessions, no home comforts, just wrought iron bedsteads with lumpy mattresses. There was a stale smell of old urine which seemed to come from the beds, and there was a small skylight on each side of the roof which let a little light in, but it gave nothing at all to look out on.

The nun made her strip naked and slowly folded her clothes as she stared at her standing there, trying to cover her modesty and her growing stomach. "Put these on!" said the nun as she threw a dark heavy cotton uniform dress, socks and underwear. Mabel quickly pulled on the ill-fitting garments and waited to be told what to do. "Follow me!" said the nun who took her back down the attic stairs but then went in a different direction and down some back stairs. Mabel could hear some noise getting closer and as a large door was thrown open, there she saw a crowd of around twenty young girls, all wearing the same type of dress as Mabel, and all bent over large washing tubs with what looked like bedding and towels in the water. There was steam everywhere and there were a few nuns who wore white tabards on top of their dark habits, barking orders at the young girls. It felt hot and sweaty as the first nun pushed her towards the head nun wearing a white tabard.

"Who's this?" she asked.

"Just came in," said the first nun and walked away.

"Go and help her!" she said, pointing to a blonde girl leaning over a large metal tub. "Go on! Now!" she screamed at Mabel who nervously hesitated. "Don't look at her," whispered the girl, "get your hands in this tub and look down!"

Mabel listened and bent over the tub, copying the girl by lifting the washing in and out and rubbing it together. "Just keep doing that for now," whispered the girl, "I'll tell you when we have to take it out and squeeze it."

"Thanks," whispered Mabel under her breath as she continued to keep her head down and look busy.

"I'm Alice," whispered the girl.

"Mabel," came the reply.

It felt like hours had passed and Mabel felt exhausted, as she was pregnant but also, she was not used to doing such heavy work. She thought she worked hard at home, but this was much harder and, to make things worse you couldn't talk or sing or do anything to make the time pass quicker, except work. At around 4.30 pm, the head nun shouted, "Right! Finish up what you're doing, scrub down your work area and head back to the refectory for dinner!" Alice started scrubbing and drying up her tub and the surrounding area. "Get that cloth and dry-up behind me, Mabel," she whispered.

"Alright, will do," said Mabel, quickly following behind her, mopping up any excess water with her cloth and rinsing it out quickly.

Once it looked clean, Alice almost stood to attention by her tub and signalled to Mabel with her eyes, to join her. The head nun approached, inspected and said to them, "You can go, and Alice, show the new girl where to go now for prayers before dinner!"

"Thank you, Sister," said Alice, taking Mabel's hand and leading her out of the laundry room. "Quick!" she said to Mabel outside of the room. "Let's get out of here!" They ran through some long underground corridors, a bit like a cellar and eventually opened a door to reveal a stone staircase which led back to a hallway drenched in natural daylight. Mabel's eyes were blinded at first by the bright light, but she rubbed them and they quickly adjusted. Alice then led her to a quiet chapel and signalled to Mabel to be quiet as they entered. There were a few nuns scattered around the chapel praying and a few girls from other jobs as well, kneeling and saying prayers. Alice pulled Mabel into a seat and knelt down, made the sign of the cross and put her head down. Mabel had been to church a few times but wasn't familiar with all the detail, so she did what she thought was the sign of the cross and knelt down beside Alice. She was trying to look devout and catholic when Alice whispered something to her.

"What?" whispered Mabel.

"Fucking fuckity fuck," whispered Alice with a huge grin on her face. Mabel was shocked and they both started giggling furiously, a combination of laughter and terror, trying not to get caught. They believed that they could conceal their laughter, but a nun a few pews behind could see their shoulders vibrating as they supposedly prayed, so she crept forward quietly and surprised them both with a hard slap to the back of their heads. Alice stopped immediately and resumed praying, but Mabel was too far gone and, despite the slap, could not stop belly laughing. She was dragged from her seat by the nun, whose angry face framed in the white headgear made Mabel even worse. As she was being hauled out of the chapel door, she realised the trouble she was in, but every time she looked at the nun, she thought of what Alice had just said and off she would go again.

It was a sharp blow to the head with a wooden object, like a walking stick, which finally stopped her laughing. She felt the blood trickle down her face and put her fingers through her thick red hair to find the wound, on the front of her scalp, not too far above her left eyebrow. "You're not laughing now, are you! The house of God is for praying, not laughing, you impudent, filthy little vagrant!" screamed the angry nun. "Now go and get cleaned up!" Just then Alice quietly emerged through the chapel door and saw the blood running down Mabel's face.

"Oh God, that was my fault, I'm so sorry. Quick, follow me!" she said quietly as she led Mabel to a little washroom with a sink and stuff for cleaning floors etc. She ran a cloth under cold water and held it over Mabel's wound. "Hopefully this will work, otherwise you'll have to get stitches from the doctor and, believe me, you don't want that!" After a few minutes of pressure, it appeared to stop bleeding.

"Thank God," said Alice. "Now let's go and get dinner!" she said as she charged down the corridor.

"No running!" screeched an elderly nun who was locking a door, so they slowed down until they were out of sight and then took off again.

The dining room was very large with long trestle-tables running the length of the room and one long table running across the width of the room, on a raised platform where the Nuns could keep an eye on the girls whilst eating their own meals. There were about 35 girls in all, some a little older, some heavily pregnant, some who had given birth and were very thin and pale. Mabel looked around the room, baffled that her life had come to this, and started to eat her vegetable stew and dry bread.

Alice disobeyed the rules and whispered to Mabel throughout the meal, telling her different people's names and stories about different nuns who were sitting eating at the top table. The senior nuns ate in a different room and the novices and other nuns sat with the girls. Suddenly, one of the dark oak doors creaked open slowly and a short man in a grey suit appeared. He made a funny noise when he walked and when she looked closely, he wore very obvious callipers on both legs, and had one very large surgical boot on his right foot. When he walked, his callipers made a squeaking noise and his shoulders swung backwards as he then forced himself forward to take the next step.

"I didn't know there were any men here, Alice?" said Mabel. "He ain't no man, He's Doctor Ross. Whatever you do, keep away from him, and if you hear his boots creaking up the stairs to the bedrooms, pretend you're snoring or he'll take you," Alice said dramatically.

"What do you mean, Alice?" said Mabel. "Use your imagination, girl. Same as why you're here, he'll do the dirty on you," she replied. "If he comes near me at night, I piss myself, cos then, he ain't interested. Why do you think the attic room stinks of piss, and when it's really bad, shit as well."

Mabel stared at Alice in disbelief. "Don't the nuns stop him?" Mabel asked. "I'll tell you this for a fact," said Alice, "there was a nice girl here last year called Theresa, and old Dr Crippen took a right shine to her, and he creaked up them bleedin' stairs one night and took her back down. She was in a terrible mess, bleeding down below, she went to Mother Superior and told her what he'd done, and Mother Superior beat her black and blue. She had to go to the hospital and say she fell down the wooden stairs and a nun never left her side so she couldn't tell the truth. She got transferred to a big asylum after that. She kept crying and screaming cos she lost her baby soon after an' all."

"Oh my God!" said Mabel. "I can't believe nuns would allow this kind of thing. I'm scared now, Alice, don't tell anyone but it was a priest did this to me." She felt the vegetable stew begin to come back up her oesophagus but took a couple of breaths and it settled down. "No!" said Alice and all Mabel could do was nod as the tears had started to fall. "Dry your eyes and don't let them see you cry, or it'll be like a free-for-all in a hen-house in this place. They'll rip you to shreds! Take my advice, keep your head down, say nothing to anyone who works here and get on with your work," said Alice, in a very determined and protective way.

"Stick with me and you'll be OK," said Alice with a wink. "You've already got my head split open today," said Mabel with a smile, and they both started to giggle.

After dinner, they had to get themselves washed for evening Benediction which was usually busy with nuns therefore harder to have any fun, however, if they chose seats close to the older nuns, they usually fell asleep so the girls could mess around for a bit. As it turned out, Alice wasn't in the same room as Mabel, but she was hatching a plan to get Mabel shifted to her room when one of her girls was due to leave the following week. They were just about to go into The

Chapel when a nun screamed, “Who is Murphy? Murphy! Show yourself!”

“I’m here, Sister!” said Mabel, holding her hand up.

“Follow me! Medical and clerking-in!” said the nun, so Mabel followed her, oblivious to what she had just said. They arrived at a door and she knocked, it was opened by a nun who looked half-dressed as a nurse with a little blue tabard with a medical cross on it as opposed to a Christian Cross. “Murphy,” said one nun to the other and she was pulled inside by the medical nun.

“Right, Murphy, I’m Sister Rose and I’m also a nurse. Unfortunately, Dr Ross has had to go out so I’ll do your weight etc and give you a physical, and you can see the doctor another time if you need to. How far gone are you?” she asked.

“Erm, they think about five months, Sister.”

“Mmmmm,” she replied, “go behind those screens and get stripped. Everything off, and then lie up on the examination bed until I get there.” Mabel stripped and lay on the cold leather examination bed without even a sheet to cover herself. Sister Rose appeared wearing gloves and carrying an enamel metal tray containing medical equipment. She put the tray down on a wooden locker and started to examine Mabel by touching her at various points of her body, without ever explaining what she was doing. When she got to Mabel’s growing stomach, she spent some time pressing from different angles and then got a small metal cone, like a trumpet and started putting it on different parts of her stomach and then putting her ear to it and listening.

“What’s that, Sister?” asked Mabel curiously.

"Shhh! No talking, I'm trying to hear the baby!" came the stern reply.

"Oh," whispered Mabel. The nun then made her open her legs wide, inserting a cold, metal speculum without warning, which made Mabel flinch with both the shock of the coldness and the discomfort. "Arghh!" she said as the nun probed and looked without permission.

"Huh!" said the nun. "If you think this is bad, just wait until it's time for it to come out of there! Then you'll know what pain is, my girl! It may have been a nice feeling when you sinned your soul, but the consequences of your sin will not be pleasant!" Mabel looked into the eyes of yet another cruel nun and thought some vicious things in her head, but she smiled and said, "Thank you, Sister. Can I get dressed now?"

"Not until you've been weighed, and your height taken, then there's a few more questions so, just be in less of a hurry and pay attention to what is happening, Murphy!"

Eventually she was released and told to go back to the Chapel as there was still 30minutes of Benediction left. "If any of the Sisters ask why you're late, tell them you've been in medical with me," said Sister Rose. Mabel was feeling very tired after such an eventful day but suddenly felt energised and realised it was when she thought about the priest and the nuns, she became frightened and angry which filled her with a measure of strength that she realised might come in handy at some point. She sneaked quietly into chapel and Alice waved and had kept a seat for her. They whispered throughout the next half-hour as the closest nuns were fast asleep and Alice informed her that she had spoken to a nun who was alright and she was going to try and get Mabel moved to the same room as her in a couple of days. "Oh, that's fantastic news," whispered Mabel. "Thank you, Alice."

As they left Chapel, Alice said, "I go this way, so I'll see you tomorrow."

"Hold on a minute, Alice," said Mabel quietly, "there's been so much happening, I ain't even asked about your baby."

"Aaaaah, I lost her 'bout four weeks ago. Miscarriage, well still-birth really, in the laundry," said Alice, becoming emotional for the first time.

"I got to seven months, so I managed to see her when she came out, before they took her away from me, and she was a beautiful little girl. Didn't even let me hold her," she whispered through her tears. Mabel hugged her tightly and shed a few tears herself, before asking, "Then why are you still here Alice?"

"They can keep you here as long as they like, and there ain't no one banging down the doors asking to take me home, so I'm stuck," said Alice as she released herself from Mabel.

"Gotta go," she said and Mabel watched her disappear down the long corridor.

5

By the following week, Mabel had been transferred to the same dormitory as Alice and seemed to have settled-in fairly well. She was a very bright girl and picked things up quickly, making her quite popular with the other girls, but still treated with suspicion and contempt by the nuns, particularly the senior nuns who seemed to hold the greatest judgement and to behave the most cruelly. The other nuns were clearly also frightened, so Mabel wondered if everyone would be much nicer if someone killed all of the old hags. She suggested it to a few girls in the dorm one night and they all started laughing. "I would love to see old Mother Superior dangling from the Chapel bell," said a girl called Mary, before saying, "God forgive me," and blessing herself.

"Too late! It's out now so God ain't forgiving you!" Mabel laughed.

"Yeah, fuck him!" said Alice angrily. "He never lifted a finger to protect me…ever! So, I don't care about his forgiveness."

Most of the girls in the upstairs rooms were pregnant, moving down to the mother and baby rooms when they delivered, but that was only if the family had agreed to have them back with the baby, which was rare. Otherwise, the girls breast fed their babies and then went to work, only coming back for their own meals and to feed their babies. They tried to avoid a bond forming as it made it harder for the girls to let the babies go when adoptive parents were found for them, and they always found someone to adopt them, or, if there was anything wrong, they would transfer the baby to the baby wards in the mental asylums and the girls would never see them again anyway. There were quite a few mothers downstairs, whose babies had already been adopted, yet they remained in the home, forced to work like slaves for their keep.

"When I've had my baby, I'm not letting anyone take it from me," said Mabel forcefully. "I'll leave with the baby and go back to Leyton with my mum and dad."

"I wish I had a guinea for every time I've heard that line," said an older girl called Janet. "I've had two babies here, one when I was fifteen and the other when I was seventeen, so I've spent a lot of time in here, and I've known a lot of the girls. I'd bet my life their ain't a single one gone out of here with their baby. Not one!"

"Bleedin' hell," said Mabel.

"Holy fuck," said Alice.

As the weeks went on, Mabel got fed-up asking the 'Sisters of No Mercy' if there were any letters from her mum or dad. She assumed they were still angry with her so kept shrugging off the sadness and loss she felt at their lack of contact. She had also started to become a bit harder because she was getting browned-off with nuns thinking that they could just strike her whenever they felt like it. She was starting to imagine the violence she would love to inflict back on them if they hit her again. She fantasised about getting

Mother Superior by the throat and strangling her until her eyes popped out. She could feel the anger coursing through her body as she thought up new ways to take revenge on the whole of the religious world as she had seen nothing but sinning and cruelty since she arrived. On one occasion, she had automatically, as a reflex, drawn back her hand to retaliate, when the perpetrating nun looked right in her eyes and said, "Go on. I dare you! I'll break every bone in your body and rip that poor little bastard out of you before you'll ever strike me!"

Mabel controlled her physical response, looked back at the nun and said, "One of these days Sister Philomena, I promise you, you'll be fucking sorry for hurting me!" She immediately saw a spark of fear in the eyes of the nun and it made her feel good.

"We'll see about that!" said the nun, but Mabel saw her fear, and it gave her more strength than she ever knew she had.

After about 12 weeks, Mabel finally got a letter from home.

Dear Mabel

I hope you are settled and behaving yourself well for the Nuns, they ought to get a medal for the wonderful work they do, where would we be without them? Sorry we haven't been in touch, but they advised us it would be too disruptive for you, so we thought it best to leave them to it.

Me and Dad and Gran, have made sure no one is gossiping, we hope, so everyone thinks you're having a great time down Southend. Sarah called at the house when you first went, but we told her we didn't know when you'd be back.

Your dad's been drunk a couple of times and tried to find that Tom, but he hasn't found him yet. He's caused this family so much trouble.

You should be due sometime soon so, hopefully they will find a family quickly and you won't have to be worrying about being a mum at your age. You're far too young.

I can't say we're not disappointed, Mabel, you've broke our hearts good and proper by messing about the way you have. I know I'm not always there for you because of my nerves, but I still can't believe that you've been doing things with boys. We never brought you up like that so we're both very hurt. I hope your time with the good Sisters will change your ways as your dad's still not sure about you coming home yet. He says you'll likely go straight back to that Tom. We'll see, Mabel. I better go and catch the post.

God bless

Mum

Mabel wept as she read the letter, heart-broken that her mum and dad believed she was to blame and were so supportive of the nuns. She felt her insides erupt as she thought of Father Cullen's attack, her beatings since coming to the convent home, the constant shaming and verbal abuse from the nuns, not to mention her raging hormones, her heartburn and the size of her belly. She knew it wasn't going to be long before the baby came and she couldn't wait for it to be over, although the nuns regularly made sure that she was never allowed to feel anything but terror around the birthing process. She read and re-read the letter several times before folding it up and putting it in her dress pocket. She groaned as she pulled herself out of the chair she was in and started looking for Alice, who was still there, as there was nowhere else to take her. Although it was a horrid place, Mabel was happy that Alice was with her and dreaded the day she would ever leave.

Mabel had been moved downstairs by this time as she couldn't get up the stairs and she couldn't lean over a tub, so she was put on sewing duties, repairing dresses and bedding which was ripped. She hated sewing but it was better than the hard physical work of the laundry, but she missed the noise and the secret laughter. When she was sewing, all she could hear was a ticking clock and an old nun's snores, hardly a match for the antics of Alice and her other friends.

It was late evening, after she had gone to bed when she felt a flood of water come from her and a searing pain began to envelop her whole body. "Jesus!" she cried as she tried to sit up. "Go get someone!" she screamed. One of the other mothers got up and ran to find the nurse. Meanwhile Mabel was in a panic as she was not prepared for the excruciating pain which had engulfed her. "Oh my good God!" she roared as she waited patiently, panting with the pain.

Then Sister Rose arrived and took over, helping Mabel to the delivery room and up onto the delivery bed, complete with wooden stirrups to hold her feet. "There's no pain relief unless things get really bad," said Sister Rose Mabel drew a deep breath inward and let out the almightiest scream as she thought she was going to explode. An assistant came in and helped the nun to prepare everything for the arrival and to put damp cloths on Mabel's forehead when she got too hot. The labour was very tough and lasted about 12 hours in all. Sister Rose wrote on Mabel's notes: "Baby Murphy was born female, at 10.33 am, weighing 7lbs 2oz by Spontaneous Vertex Delivery." Which means normal delivery.

Mabel was more exhausted than she had ever felt before, however, she was still eager to see her daughter, but her baby was quickly removed from the delivery room by Sister Rose and taken to the Nursery. "I wanna see my baby," she said to the assistant who was still mopping her brow.

"You'll have to wait," said the young Novice anxiously, followed by "Get some sleep now while you can." But Mabel's mind was racing, wondering about her baby, where were they taking her and, were they giving her away right now? Her heart started racing and her maternal instincts became strong as she pushed her way up from the ned and swung her weak legs over the side.

"Where's my fucking baby?" she screamed at the Novice as she slipped off the bed and onto her feet, pulling her nightdress down and heading for the door.

"Please now, don't!" said the anxious Novice. "Come and lie down again please?" But Mabel was in wounded mother mode and stomped down the corridors calling, "Sister Rose! Where are you?" But there was no response. She saw a door with a small sign which said Nursery and barged in, but there were only two girls feeding their babies.

"You seen Sister Rose?" asked Mabel frantically but they both shook their heads. She returned to the corridors, wondering where on earth they could have taken her. "Mother Superior!" she screamed as her rage drove her at speed through the corridors, telling Nuns to "fuck off!" if they told her to stop running.

She burst into the room and Mother Superior screamed, "What is the meaning of this!" but the scene spoke for itself.

Sister Rose holding her baby and showing it to a young couple who were sitting in the bay window, looking so excited to be having a baby.

"That's my fucking baby, now give her here!" Mabel screamed.

The couple looked shocked, and as Mother Superior began to shout, "Get out of here."

Mabel turned to look at her directly and said venomously, "If you don't shut that nasty fuckin mouth of yours, I'll shut it for you, you evil old cunt!" Mother Superior, possibly for the first time in her life, was dumbstruck, and ran out of the room calling for assistance.

"Give her to me!" she spat at Sister Rose who nervously handed the baby over to her mother. Mabel began to cry and held her daughter tight, sitting down in an empty chair next to the couple. "Hello darlin'," she whispered through her tears, "I'm your mum," and she rocked back and forth, sobbing and wondering how long before they stole her back.

It wasn't long before the head nun was back with reinforcements. "Take that baby off her and get her out of here!" she yelled. She then rushed to her large wooden desk and lifted some documents which she held in the air. "My baby, I think you'll find young lady!" she said, trying to appear 'in control' for the benefit of the couple. "Signed by both your parents I might add!" she said with glee.

Mabel reluctantly passed the baby back to Sister Rose and felt her fight and energy leave her. "When are you taking her?" she asked the young couple.

"We were hoping sometime next week?" said the young woman desperately.

"Do something for me, will you?" said Mabel.

"Anything," said the woman. "Don't let them give her to you unless I'm there. I wanna be able to say goodbye to my little girl." She sobbed.

"Of course," said the young woman. "And thank you for giving us such a precious gift," she added. Mother Superior snapped her fingers and two Nuns and a male gardener escorted Mabel out of the office. As they reached the door, Mother said through gritted teeth, "Murphy. I will deal with you later," just to ensure there was even more fear instilled in a child of fourteen who had just had a baby.

As good as their word, ten days later the couple came to pick up the baby which Mabel had called Elizabeth, after her mum. She had been allowed to see her a few times, but they kept her away as much as possible, mainly as punishment for the things she said in the office, in front of the new parents. Mabel was presentable and fresher looking as she held her daughter one last time. "Now you be a good girl," she said as she kissed her forehead.

"I've called her Elizabeth, but you'll want to change it I expect," said Mabel to her baby's new mother.

"Oh, it can be her middle name if that's alright," said the woman.

"I would like that, thank you," said Mabel as she felt the floods of tears rushing out of her eyes. Mabel was escorted back to her bedroom on the other side of the building before they left as the Sisters didn't like emotional scenes taking place in the grounds as babies were being removed, or mothers banging the windows as they drove off.

"Much less histrionics this way," Mother Superior said to the couple. "Better for everyone." Then she waved, as the black car drove out towards the gates.

Back in the laundry, Mabel was trying to stop crying and trying not to dwell on what had just happened, but her mind wouldn't let her. She could see Father Cullen smiling because he got away with it and she wondered, how many more there were like her. She thought of her beautiful baby and hoped that the young couple would love and look after her. She thought about this horrible place, and how so much violence and cruelty came from women who were supposed to be kind and compassionate. So far, she had only met one nun who was remotely nice, but that nun was being bullied herself by the others, so maybe she knew how it felt and couldn't bring herself to join them.

Mabel had heard some of the other girls say, "The good ones always leave," and in that moment she felt that she knew why that was. They did have a true vocation to serve God but then you are sent to a place where, over time, most of the Nuns have become angry, controlling and very unhappy individuals who make themselves feel better by abusing and denigrating others. The ones who stay, either have to become like them or join their victims. Finally, despite the horror and the trauma, it all made sense.

6

After a few weeks, Mabel had settled back into her old room with Alice and the other girls and was enjoying being back in the laundry. Although it was very tough work, it made the days pass quicker and, so long as you were doing your work and weren't skiving, the nuns in the laundry tended to enjoy a quiet life so there was less shouting and markedly less physical violence. Mabel was posted close to Alice so they could still whisper and chat and have a quiet giggle. Alice was very funny and often fearless in the risks she took just to make us laugh. She would bend over bags of dirty linen and would call out a swearword loudly. Everyone would begin to have shocked laughter as the half-asleep nuns would shout, "What was that?" in disbelief that they had heard the word 'Fuck' in their laundry. "Never heard anything, Sister," would come the reply from Alice. Unsure of facts, the nun would shout, "Look! Just get on with your work and less of the chit chatting!" and all the girls would be hanging over their tubs pretending to work but helpless with laughter.

"You're gonna get us all killed, Alice!" said Mabel through her laughter. "It's the only think keeping me going in this god-forsaken place," said Alice.

"Getting one over on those old hags," Mabel knew exactly what she meant and nodded her head in agreement.

Later that morning, a novice appeared and called out, "Murphy! Doctor!" and stood waiting at the door. Mabel looked at Alice with a shocked and terrified expression. "Oh Gawd," said Alice. "Listen, Mabel, if it don't feel right, don't let him do it."

"But how?" said Mabel, feeling panicked.

"You'll know if it happens," said Alice wisely. "I haven't got all day Murphy!" shouted the nun from the door. "Coming, Sister," said Mabel, rushing forward to meet her. As they entered Dr Ross' office, he was seated behind his large wooden desk which made him look even smaller. "Thank you, Sister," he said, and the escorting nun left the room.

"Now then," he said as he looked across the desk at Mabel. "How did I manage to miss your admission examination, young lady? I don't remember you at all," he said.

"I see you've had your baby and its adopted, so let's just have a look at you and see that everything is healing up normally, shall we?" He drew the screens back and asked her to undress and lay on the bed which, being a male, made her feel very frightened and shameful, however, she did what he asked and lay down on the bed. Dr Ross appeared wearing no gloves and with no tray of equipment.

"I'm just going to do a quick head to toe and then we'll have a look at your cervix etc. He gently touched her around her neck glands then went straight to her breasts which were still tender and sometimes still leaking milk. He spent a long time on each breast which made Mabel feel uncomfortable, but she wasn't brave enough to challenge him, so she remained silent. He then palpated her abdomen for a few minutes before moistening his fingers with some petroleum jelly and reaching down towards her vagina."

"No need for any equipment today, just a little feel around," he said, as he inserted two fingers. Mabel was in full blown panic and, as on previous occasions, felt frozen and unable to fight back. She had her eyes closed, hoping it would soon be over when she heard the doctor make a quiet groaning sound, similar to that of Father Cullen. She opened her eyes and saw that his free hand was in his white coat pocket, vigorously moving back and forth. Her body filled with uncontrollable rage at the thought that this could be happening again. She drew back her arm and slapped him as hard as she could, across his face, knocking off his small round wire spectacles and causing him to lose his balance, but he managed to save himself by holding on to the bed by her feet. She didn't even think about it. She drew back her right leg and slammed him in the face with the base of her foot, knocking him to the floor. She shot up from the bed and pulled her clothes back on as he struggled to get back up due to his callipers and surgical boot. She looked at him with raging eyes and said, "I'm reporting you to Mother Superior, you dirty little fucker!"

"She won't believe you, I was only doing my job as a doctor," he protested nervously.

"Well, I know all about you, Dr Crippen, and I'm gonna put a stop to it!" she yelled as she drew back her leg and kicked him square in the face. He fell back down, and blood began to pour on to the polished floor. "I'm watching you now!" said Mabel as she slammed his office door behind her.

Before she could settle down or change her mind, she burst into Mother Superiors Office. "What's the meaning of this!" she yelled as she tried to swallow the jam scone which she had in her mouth. "Get out of here!" she insisted.

"I'm going nowhere until you hear me out and do something about that filthy, so-called doctor you got working here!" said Mabel, fearlessly Mother Superior stood up to try and feel more superior.

"Doctor Ross is a fine, Christian man and an excellent doctor!" she screamed. "How dare you come in here."

"Shut the fuck up!" said Mabel in her fury. "And listen!"

"You will not tell me what to do, Murphy!" she said as she headed for the door to call for reinforcements, but Mabel was quicker to the door, turned the key and took it out.

"You're going nowhere 'till you hear me out!" said Mabel, holding up the large heavy key. "Now sit on your fat lazy arse and shut the fuck up!" She could see the combination of rage and fear in the nun's eyes as she slowly obeyed the command and sat down at her desk.

Mabel took a deep breath and said, "I ain't a whore or a slut. I was raped by my local priest whilst my mum lay ill in the next room. I was a girl and didn't know anything about what was happening to me. I didn't know about sex! Or babies! Next thing I know I'm here. Getting kicked like a dog every day from you people! People who are supposed to be good!"

The nun was extremely uncomfortable but unrepentant about the facts which were pouring forth from a young girl's mouth. "When I got here, I was actually quite excited to be getting, so-called help from the Sisters, but I was here for less than 12 hours when a nun split my head open with a walking stick!" she continued.

"That's when all the other girls told me not to go to the doctor as he touches you up and asks you to do unspeakable things. So, I stopped the bleeding myself, rather than risk another man having his way with me!"

"This is nonsense, coming from a child who sits with the devil!" she screamed.

"I told you to shut the fuck up 'til I'm finished," said Mabel as she slapped her hard, on the side of the head, knocking her back into her chair.

"I won't ask you again," said Mabel menacingly, as she saw the confidence drain-away from her tormentor. "Then, just now, I'm dragged to that little monster's office for a medical. Just me and him, no chaperone, nothing! He strips me naked and starts doing things to me, pretending like that's how things are done when you get examined, but I knew it weren't right! No gloves, no tray of medical things, just his bare hands doing what they wanted! He'll be here soon, no doubt, to report me, but I'm getting in first. He had one hand inside me and one hand pleasuring himself, and you call me a dirty whore? What does that make him Mother Superior?" she creamed into her face.

Mother superior appeared to have gathered some strength as she stood up and appeared to instigate a sort of 'survival plan B'. "Give me the key, girl," she said quietly, hoping that it may calm Mabel down.

"Let's sort this out and get back to normal." Mabel was confused by the tone and content of her speech. "I've listened to your complaints and I will investigate and get things sorted, but just give me the key so that you can go back to your room and I can get started. Mabel felt her body slow down and she handed over the key which Mother Superior snatched and ran to the door, turning it in the lock."

"I need some assistance here! Quickly!" called the nun as she re-entered the room wearing her old familiar expression.

"You'll be sorry for what you've done today! Very sorry indeed!" she yelled. The open door was pushed further, and she knew by the squeaking noises that it was Dr Ross who stood at the other side. "Doctor, I'm afraid this evil child has made some outlandish claims about you, which I neither believe nor intend to even acknowledge. When the others arrive, she will be moved to the side-room which we keep for violent behaviour, and she'll stay there until I decide what's best for her."

She turned to look directly at Mabel and said, "You ARE a whore! A violent, ignorant whore! Your parents were glad to see the back of you, because of the shame you brought on them, and you tell me that you are good, and we are all bad? You are deluded my girl!" Just then, like an animal who is playing dead, waiting for the right moment to escape from a family of lions, Mabel jumped up and ran towards the grand, decorative open fireplace and grabbed a heavy iron poker with an extra spike which stuck out of the side of the shaft. She drew in a deep breath and screamed as she ran towards the Mother Superior with the poker above her head and swung it hard, hitting the nuns back and causing her to scream with the pain, but Mabel wasn't finished, she swung the heavy poker back around and hit her in the stomach this time, which made her bend forward and fall to the floor in a heap.

"Get the Police!" she called as Mabel aimed her final blow to the back of her head which both shut her up and started her blood flowing. Some of the other nuns arrived and said, "You've killed her! You'll be sorry now."

"Shut the fuck up or you'll be next!" said Mabel. "She ain't dead, I can hear her snoring like she does in Church!"

Sister Clara, who was a carbon copy of Mother Superior stepped forward. "Put that poker down now and get yourself to the side-room before the police get here!" she said.

"Do you want to end up lying there beside her?" said Mabel. "Well, fuck off and mind your own business!" She knew that her choices were limited, and that the punishment would be severe, either here or if she was taken to prison. She held the poker like a lethal weapon and told the gathering crowd to back up and let her out. They were temporarily stunned and were not sure what to do without their leader barking orders at them, so they slowly moved backwards and let Mabel through.

"If any of you follow me, you'll get the same as her," she threatened as she turned and ran up the corridor and out into the grounds. She knew the Police would arrive via the front gate, so she ran into the trees and followed the perimeter wall for a while, before she found a section she could climb. She threw the poker into the long grass and climbed the seven-foot wall, lying flat on top until she could orientate herself and see which way to go. She saw a small building in the distance and felt it better to go in that direction rather than into town, where everyone will be looking for her.

It was grey-dark, so soon she would be able to hide for the night, she thought. As she got closer to the house, she realised it was a small dairy farm with some outbuildings at the back, so she crept around the main building and found a way into the cowshed where several black and white cows were lying down. A few of them made a little noise when she arrived but they soon settled. She saw a small area, slightly cordoned off in the corner so she headed over there to make her camp for the night.

She made a makeshift bed with hay and built it up higher on one side so that if anyone came in, they wouldn't notice her. She lay there, looking at the wooden roof and suddenly came back to earth with a bump.

"Oh God, what have I done?" she asked herself as she started to shake and sob uncontrollably. "I'm for it now, I've killed a nun, I'll be all over the front pages. I'll go to prison. Mum and Dad will never take me back now." She sobbed, until eventually, she was all cried out and fell asleep.

She awoke with the cockerel crowing in the next barn and quickly sat up, not quite sure of where she was. "What do we have here then?" said an older grey-haired man, sitting on a small stool milking a cow.

"Sorry, sir," said Mabel, flustered and taken aback. "I got lost and just came in for a bit of shelter."

"That's alright love, no harm done," he said. "You from the convent?"

"Erm, yeah, I was visiting someone I know," said Mabel who was a hopeless liar.

"Was it you who hit the old one?" he asked with a smile on his face, Mabel didn't know how to respond or what he was thinking. "About time someone gave her a slap I'd say. It's been a long time coming!" he said as he threw his head back in laughter. She smiled at him nervously, delighted that he agreed with her behaviour.

"You wanna bit of breakfast love?" he asked.

"There's just me and the wife, so you'll be safe enough for now."

"Yes, please," said Mabel. "And thank you," she said.

"Don't thank me, darlin', you ain't tasted my wife's cooking yet!" He roared and laughed his head off again. Mabel felt safe for the first time in months and smiled back as he cackled to himself.

As they entered the kitchen Mabel could smell the most amazing aromas of bacon and eggs and homemade bread. "This is Mavis and I'm Tom," said the farmer introducing his wife who turned from the cooking range and said, "Good morning, my love, wash your hands and sit yourself down, we've plenty to go 'round."

"Thank you, I'm Mabel," she replied, washing her hands at the small sink. "We saw you late last night and didn't want to frighten you," said Mavis. "They did come to the door looking for you later in the evening, they always come here first, but we said we hadn't seen anyone."

"Oh, thank you," said Mabel. "You're not the first and you won't be the last from that place," said Mavis, "and they all tell the same story, so it can't be a lie, can it?" Mabel felt such relief at their support and got stuck into the huge breakfast, as if she hadn't eaten for weeks.

"Problem is, you can't stay on here love," said Tom, "they would catch you for sure and then me and the wife would be in prison for hiding you. Aiding and abetting it's called."

"I understand," said Mabel with a sigh of despair. "But don't worry, we'll do what we did for all the rest. Mavis will do a lovely picnic lunch to take with you and you can have a few coppers and a different set of clothes, then I'll drop you in Maidstone as I'm going into the Market," said Tom proudly. “You can decide what you want to do from there, but you won’t be so conspicuous.”

Mavis sat down next to her and took her hand. “Listen, love,” she said. “We’ve lived here for many years, and you can’t ignore the screams and unhappiness that comes from that place. We see the poor souls being taken in and we see the flashy cars driving out every week with babies. We ain’t stupid love. So, when we get the opportunity to help one of you poor girls, we bloody well do!” And she squeezed Mabel’s hand tightly. “When you’re ready, there’s a dress and cardigan and jacket in my room there. May be a little big, but they’ll do a turn and I’ll get rid of your stuff so they can’t never find it,” she said. “Now I’d better get your lunch sorted, hadn’t I?”

“Thank you so very much,” said Mabel.

“I was starting to think there were no nice people left in the world.”

Around mid-morning, Tom said, “Alright, love, coast is clear, we had better make a move.”

“There’s a lovely bit of food in this bag for you and two shillings which will get you a train ticket back home if you need it. Take good care love and know that we are thinking of you,” said Mavis as she hugged her tight.

“Thanks for everything,” said Mabel. “I can’t thank you enough.”

As they drove past the gates to the home, she looked and saw life continuing as usual. “Do you think I killed her?” she asked Tom.

“You couldn’t kill her except with a silver bullet!” he said as he threw his head back laughing. “She’s as right as rain love, the people who came last night told me. Although you did give her a fair whack mind you, and she'll have a sore head this morning, that's for sure!" Mabel smiled at him and wished she could have stayed with them forever, but she knew that he was right. They weren't going to let her away with assaulting the head nun and if they could get her brought back for them to punish, that would be the icing on the cake for Mother Superior, but what was she going to do. She thought about going home but the police would probably be waiting for her and her mum and dad weren't really speaking to her anyway so she felt like she did not have many choices open to her. She saw the buildings begin to change and knew she must be arriving in Maidstone.

"Shall I drop you at the station love?" asked Tom kindly.

"Yes, please, Tom," she replied. "And thank you to both of you for helping me so much."

"That's no bother, my love," he said as he walked her up to the station doors. "Goodbye, girl," he said with a smile.

"Goodbye," said Mabel as she entered the station and started to panic about what to do next.

"I don't know where to go," she said to the ticket-master.

"Well, that's a nice problem to have, love," he replied with a smile, "but there's a queue behind you, and they know where they're going so can you let them through, please?"

"Sorry!" she said as she stepped aside to let them through. She looked up at the old arrivals and departures board and, for some reason, she just decided she was going home.

"Single to London Bridge please," she said. "That's one shilling and tuppence please," replied the officer, stamping her ticket with the printing machine. "Platform two at 11.00 am!" he said and took her money.

Mabel was both excited and full of fear. Would her mum and dad be happy to see her or would they be angry with her? What would she do if they rejected her, where could she go? She thought about her nan, Beryl, and wondered if she would help her if she didn't have a good result at her own house. She was sure that her nan would be understanding as she had helped look after her mum for years and had a very kind heart. She went to the platform to wait for her train and was hopeful that the next episode of her adventure would be happier than the most recent one.

She sat on the polished wooden bench and looked across to the other platforms, wondering where people were going to, couples, adults and children, all with different sized luggage, some dressed smartly, some dressed more casually. It was whilst sitting daydreaming that she suddenly saw two police officers on the other platform and, when she looked at the entrance to her own platform, she saw another two coming down the stairs. She began to panic and looked for somewhere to escape or hide, and she saw a small waiting room with wooden benches. She ran inside but immediately heard a police whistle and male voices calling, "You girl! Stop!" She began shaking and had nowhere to escape to, so she sat on a wooden bench with her head down and felt completely broken.

The door to the witing room was pushed open and the larger police officer looked at her and said, "Mabel Murphy?"

She knew the game was over before it had started and said, "Yes, sir, I'm Mabel Murphy."

"I'm arresting you for a serious assault on Mother Superior at the Sisters of Mercy mother and baby home. Now come with me and no more of your shenanigans, young lady."

7

Mabel arrived in a small Police Station near Maidenhead and was escorted into a small reception area manned by an older Police Officer. "This is Mabel Murphy from the Convent," said the arresting officer. "Put her in a cell until I sort out what we're doing with her."

"Yes, Sarge, will do!" said the desk-officer, and he escorted her through a door and downstairs to a cellar which contained three small, dark cells. "In you go," said the officer as he held open a heavy cell door.

"I'm really scared," said Mabel, beginning to feel vulnerable at the thought of being locked up.

"Well," said the officer with a knowing look. "Maybe you should have thought about that before you clumped an old nun with an iron poker." He slammed the heavy door shut and left Mabel alone, in a small, cold and smelly cell with only a small metal-framed bed bolted into the ground. She lay down on the bed and began to sob, despite her best efforts, she was trapped and would be punished by the authorities for violence against a nun.

After a couple of hours, she heard doors unlocking and footsteps approaching her cell. The key was turned in her lock and there stood the arresting officer, Sergeant Maitland. "OK, young lady, you will appear in front of the magistrate tomorrow charged with the assault of the Holy Mother. You will be asked to give an account of the incident and then he will decide what's best for you. Do you understand?" he said firmly.

"Yes, sir," said Mabel anxiously, "will they send me to prison?"

"Truth is, I really don't know, girl. You're still very young and it all depends how the Magistrate feels. I think you'll be seeing Mr Bradbury-Brown who may be a bit more lenient than some of the others. How did you get yourself into this pickle?" he asked, showing the first hint of humanity.

His empathy made Mabel burst out crying. "Oh, I don't know." She sobbed. "One minute everything was happy, then everything came tumbling down. I'm a good girl, Sergeant."

"Well, let's hope he feels the same tomorrow," he said. "Now I'll be back with some of that nice food from your bag for you. Don't want it going to waste now do we, and you need to get some sleep ready for the court."

Next morning Mabel was escorted to Courtroom number one in a large building a few miles away, probably Maidstone, she thought. It was quite a large room with wooden seats like Church Pews and a raised area which had a large throne-like chair. There was a couple of official looking people sitting down writing notes and a few members of the public sitting observing. She wondered if the Police would have brought her parents and prayed that, by some miracle, they were suddenly going to appear, but she knew they had no real way of contacting them and, even if they did, it would be unlikely that they would have been able to travel.

“All rise for Mr Bradbury Brown!” called one of the officials, and in walked an older gentleman dressed in fancy robes who walked up the steps and took his place on the throne.

“Be seated!” he said as he looked at the papers in front of him. He slowly lifted his head and fixed his stare directly onto Mabel, before slowly looking back at his papers. “What exactly do you have to say for yourself, Miss Murphy!” he bellowed at her.

“You hit an elderly nun several times with a heavy poker and left her seriously injured! What do you have to say for yourself then? Speak up!”

Mabel’s by now familiar inability to communicate and uncontrollable shaking began and, the more she tried to justify herself, the deeper the trouble became. “So you were, in fact, being cared for by these nuns because you were with child?” he roared. “You assaulted the very people who were trying to take care of you when you clearly could not take care of yourself? Where is your sense of right and wrong girl? Promiscuity and biting the hand that feeds you when you were receiving their charitable care? I just don’t understand!”

“I’m sorry, sir, I just want to go home, I didn’t mean to hurt anyone, I swear I didn’t,” she pleaded. “I just want to go home.”

“Well, I can assure you that you will not be going home for some time young lady,” he said. “Although I am a fair and lenient man, I will not be sending you to prison. I fear that your morals and behaviour fall seriously short of what is expected in a Christian society and I am concerned that these loose morals may be passed-on to other young girls whom you come into contact with. You pose a serious moral threat to the public; therefore, I am committing you to the South East London Asylum for your own care and protection and the protection of others. You will be held there until the Medical Authorities decide that you are fit to live safely without psychiatric care!"

Mabel felt as if she was out of her body, having a dream, and looking down on the courtroom. She could hear noisy echoes and loud voices but she couldn't seem to translate any sounds into sensible language. She saw the magistrate moving his mouth and banging his wooden hammer, but she was lost in what was happening. A Police officer grabbed her arm and led her out of court and into an official car on the street outside. "What's happening?" she asked the Police Officer as she was being bundled in to back seat.

"You're going to the looney bin!" he said with a smug smile as he got into the front of the car. Mabel had heard her Nan berating people who called Claybury Asylum the looney bin, and she suddenly filled with fear and dread. She had visited her mum there many times and was absolutely shocked that anyone would think she deserved to be a patient in one of these places. She could hear the two officers in the front seat sniggering and laughing as they drove away and started heading for Surrey.

As the car slowly navigated the road which followed the outline of the high walls and overhanging trees, she saw the very grand entrance gate which had heavy wrought iron gates hanging from decorative stone pillars with a small gate lodge where a member of staff came out and asked for paperwork. The policeman driving handed him the signed court documentation which the gate-keeper read and began to give directions on how to get to 'The Female Block'.

Through the opening gates Mabel could see an enormous, three-storey building which seemed to go on forever. There was a circular road which went to the main entrance, a very ornate frontage with climbing ivy and large windows, but the car drove past to the left and followed a road for several hundred yards until they reached a sign which said 'Female Wards'. The car pulled up and she was led through a large blue door into a huge corridor with doors leading off signed A1, A2, A3, then B1, B2, B3. They stopped at E block and walked up one flight of stairs to E2 and knocked the door which had a small window through which Mabel could see women jumping up and down screaming and Nurses in uniform trying to control them.

The door was unlocked by a large middle-aged nurse with her hair scraped up into a bun, topped with her starched white hat. "Yes?" she said abruptly.

"New admission from the court, here's the paperwork," said the Police officer.

"Oh, fuck this!" said the nurse. "I'm almost on capacity and I ain't got no staff!" She snatched the paperwork from his hand and signalled for Mabel to enter. "Sit there and don't move!" she said as she slammed the door on the escorts, handed Mabel the paperwork and ran back to the commotion in the dining area with two female patients. Mabel was frightened but remained calm. She saw the nurses restraining one of the women as the middle-aged nurse appeared with a glass syringe which, without removing any clothing, she stuck into the patient's behind and pushed the plunger.

Very soon there was silence and the nurse with the needle looked at the other screaming woman and said aggressively, "You want some as well?"

The female patients became tearful and began shaking her head. "Don't want the needle! Don't want the needle!" she said.

"Well get in to your bed right now or you'll be bloody next!" said the exasperated nurse.

During the chaos, Mabel had discreetly looked down at the official paperwork she was holding and, despite being a slow reader, she could see her name and date of birth at the top of the page and her address was written as the convent. She was puzzled that her address wasn't Leyton and wanted to ask the nurse, but now was not the time. Next to her details and 'Emergency Hospitalisation' was a box which said 'Diagnosis' and in the Magistrate's hand was written 'Moral Defective' Mabel had no idea what any of it meant but guessed it must be serious for her to have gotten into so much trouble that she was locked in an asylum beside such scary people.

"Don't you dare read anything in this ward!" screamed the nurse as she slapped Mabel on the side of the head, which gave her a real shock, so much so, that she shouted, "Oi!" before she could stop herself. The nurse bent over her slowly and said, "I'm Sister Jeffries and I run this ward! Don't you ever fucking 'Oi' me again, or you'll know all about it! Now get into that office and sit on your behind until I get to you!"

Mabel stood up and flounced into the small open door with 'Sister' written on a wooden plaque. She was beginning to become comfortable with feeling angry and as she sat on the wooden chair, she looked out at the ward and said, "Fucking fat cow." Not loud enough for anyone to hear, but loud enough to make her feel a bit better, in fact she couldn't prevent a little smirk from appearing as she reflected on what she had just said.

Within a short space of time, she was examined, weighed, measured, stripped, bathed, re-dressed in horrible hospital-issue clothing, fed some awful stew and told which bed in the dormitory belonged to her. It was a whirlwind of a day and Mabel felt quite disorientated and confused. Sister Jeffries approached her with a small pot containing some pills and said, "Open!"

"Sorry, Sister," said Mabel.

"Open your bleedin' mouth, you halfwit!" screamed the nurse.

"What is it for Sister?" asked Mabel fearfully.

"Never you mind what it's for, Missy! Let's just say it's helps people not to attack helpless nuns!" replied the Sister with a level of glee and another uncontainable smirk.

Mabel felt her anger rise and thought about her mum's time spent in Claybury, when she was filled with several strong drugs for weeks at a time and could hardly speak. "I don't want it," said Mabel defiantly.

"You're bloody well having it you little cow!" said Sister Jeffries as she attempted to lean over Mabel but before she could do anything, Mabel had kicked the little pot out of her hand and smacked her right across the face, knocking her sideways onto an armchair. "You little bitch!" said the Sister, shocked that Mabel had got the better of her.

"Fuck off!" shouted Mabel as she dodged a couple of other nurses and ran into the dormitory area to try to escape. There were two sets of doors which went into the dormitory, one from the dayroom area and one from the dining area. She could hear shouting and footsteps behind her and saw a door at each side at the far end of the forty bedded room. She tried the one on the right but it was locked so she quickly sprinted to the left door which was unlocked and she ran through it and discovered she was on an enclosed bridge which connected to the next block. D2 was written on the door at the end of the bridge but as she turned the handle, it was locked. Her anger was now being overtaken by fear as she turned around and saw Sister Jeffries with two other nurses approaching fast.

"You are going to be one sorry fucking lady!" said the angry Sister with the red hand mark across her left cheek.

"You'll regret the day you ever clapped eyes on me!" Within seconds, Mabel had been punched, slapped, kicked and dragged to the ground by her hair, then dragged across the floor back to the ward. "Put her into seclusion and make sure she's in bed restraints!" screamed the sister.

"If she doesn't want tablets, I'll give her a much stronger drug in a much more painful way!"

Mabel was dragged into a small room, similar to the police cell she had spent the night in, and was held onto a cast iron bed while thick leather buckle restraints were fastened around her arms and legs and attached to the bed frame. She couldn't move at all and was panting after all of the exertion so she just stopped fighting. Her body became limp and she stopped screaming. Sister Jeffries arrived with a metal 'kidney dish' and asked one of the nurses to hold it whilst she filled the syringe. "This lovely drug here is called Paraldehyde, have you ever heard of it?" she asked menacingly. Mabel ignored her and just looked at the size of the syringe and needle. "I've chosen this drug because its thick and oily, which means it will be very painful for your muscle to absorb it! I've also chosen a very thick needle which will make it very painful, and thirdly, it stinks! You will smell like a skunk in season because you're gonna be out of action for around two days, during which time you WILL shit and piss yourself young lady. It won't be a pretty sight, but out of all this madness you'll remember one thing…Don't fuck with Sister Jeffries!" Then, as quick as a flash, the thick needle was embedded in her upper thigh and she let out a blood-curdling scream as Sister Jeffries kept moving the needle from side to side an in and out in order to cause maximum discomfort.

The next thing Mabel remembered was waking up and, just as the crazy nurse had promised, she was doubly incontinent, still in restraints and her mouth was so dry her lips were stuck together. She slowly looked around the small room and got her bearings. She was alone and the door had a spy-hole. She heard it opening and saw an eyeball looking through.

"You awake then?" asked whoever owned the eyeball.

Mabel nodded her head and made the noise, "Mmmm," because she couldn't unstick her lips, they felt crusty and sore. The smell of her own excrement, mixed with the heavy aroma of paraldehyde was disgusting and was making her feel sick.

At that moment, a key turned in the lock and there stood Sister Jeffries, resplendent in a clean navy-blue uniform, white starched apron, white shoes and starched white hat. She wore a silver fob-watch on her right breast pocket and a badge, scissors, a black and a red pen in her left breast pocket. She slowly walked into the seclusion room like a captain inspecting his troops.

"What do we have here then?" she asked, as if she had no idea what was going on. She picked up the corner of a sheet and looked at the mess, raised her eyebrows and said, "Oh, dear me, looks like this little clever-clogs can't hold her bottom shut. Are you getting that awful smell?" she said, loudly, trying to monopolise on the shame.

"Have you got anything to say shitty arse?" said the Sister, feeling a little bit of power.

"Not really, fat-arse!" said Mabel as her lips began to loosen. "Only that it seems to be the drug and the huge syringe which caused all of this and I will report everything that you've done to me, to your boss this week!"

The Sister was losing her cockiness and said, "What do you want to complain about? You've had a lovely time with us, haven't you?" But Mabel was no longer scared. She saw a glint of fear in Jeffries eyes and this gave her strength.

"Just you wait and fucking see what I'm gonna do!" said Mabel as she stared into her eyes and smiled confidently. "Right!" said Jeffries to her nurses. "Get her up and bathed and get this room cleaned up immediately!"

As Mabel was escorted past her, she deliberately rubbed-up against her and, with an intimidating smile said, "Oh, sorry, Sister Jeffries, I think I got some of my shit on your clean uniform!"

Jeffries was furious, but was beginning to see that Mabel wasn't going to 'break' as easily as the others. She began to think about what might happen if she gained any power within the patient population and this really scared her. 23 years she had been working in this Asylum and she wasn't about to let a slip of a girl get the better of her. The battle lines were being drawn up by them both but she realised that, unlike her, Mabel had nothing left to lose so didn't care.

8

Over the next few days there developed what seemed to be a 'ceasefire' between Sister Jeffries and Mabel and they simply 'danced around each other' but said and did nothing to upset the other. Mabel had also started to get to know some of the other patients. There was Theresa who had also been in the mother and baby several years back and had never recovered from her baby being taken away. She suffered with psychosis and often heard her baby crying for her which pushed her into a hysterical state. She was one of the screaming ladies on Mabel's arrival, but now that they were chatting, she realised that there wasn't much wrong with her except the damage which years in the asylum had done. Mabel became so angry that, yet another life had been destroyed by the Nuns, and vowed that she wasn't going to become another Theresa.

There was also Margaret who had schizophrenia and every so often she would stop doing whatever she was doing and would have a full conversation with someone only she could see and hear. When Mabel asked, "Who are you talking to Margaret?" she replied, "My grandfather. He's dead but visits me every day."

"What does he talk about?" asked Mabel curiously.

"Oh, just the usual, but sometimes he upsets me because he calls me bad names and I don't like it." Mabel felt bad for all the other women in the unit and began to feel responsible for making sure they were treated fairly. She felt that, even though she was only 15, she had a duty to take care of those worse off than her. She was used to visiting her mum and seeing people with mental illness struggle, so she wanted to make things better for them.

Within a couple of weeks, Mabel knew everyone and felt quite comfortable in the ward, having a good idea of which staff were good and which were a threat. The staff team led by Sister Jeffries were the worst and when they were on duty there was much more chaos and people being drugged, and on another team, there were some quieter older nurses who were very kind and thoughtful. The night staff could be a problem as they liked to have a sleep, and if someone was 'playing-up', they were short tempered and tended to use the needle as a deterrent. One of these nurses was known simply as 'Johnstone' and she was a cranky, short-tempered older woman. She was very aloof and would never engage in conversation with patients as she believed herself to be above them. She also only used surnames when addressing anyone, patients or staff, and was extremely 'unemotional' and 'matter-of-fact' in her communication. "Murphy, get to bed" or "Murphy, shut up" were about the only words she ever had directed at her, although, in some ways Mabel was happier knowing exactly how someone was, rather than the manipulative, duplicitous behaviour of some people.

When Matron toured the blocks, everyone looked perfect and all that could be heard was "Yes, Matron" and "No, Matron" which really annoyed Mabel as some of them were so awful when she wasn't around, but she knew who they were and knew not to trust them.

It was during one of those visits when Matron looked at Mabel and said, "And who are you?"

"I'm Mabel Murphy, Matron," she replied.

"Can you read and write, Mabel?" asked Matron.

"I can, Matron, sometimes a little slowly if it's difficult words, but I get there," said Mabel honestly.

"Interesting," said Matron. "I might have a job for you, Mabel Murphy," she said with a smile and a wink. "Report to my office tomorrow at 9.00 and I will let you know what I want. I'll let Sister Jeffries know you'll be coming over."

"Thank you, Matron!" said Mabel excitedly.

She watched Matron go into the office and saw Sister turn and look at her when Matron told her the news. She knew that Sister Jeffries would be very upset, but she also knew it gave Mabel a little more power over her and that she would be less likely to be cruel to her, although she also had concerns for the weaker patients. She felt confident that she could maintain some sort of balance back on the ward, because of her new connection with Matron.

"Don't be getting any ideas above your station, Murphy!" said Sister the next day as Mabel was leaving for her appointment. "Once she realises you're a liability, she'll march you back here quicker than when you came in!" and she opened the door and released Mabel into the staircase which led to the long corridors.

"Follow the corridor opposite D Block and that will take you to admin-block. You'll find Matron's office on the first floor," she said before slamming and locking the door.

Mabel walked up the carpeted staircase with shiny brass rods holding the dark green carpet firmly on each stair. On the first floor were two doors. One said, 'Committee Room' in gold lettering, the other said simply 'Matron'. She knocked on the door and, after a few seconds the door was opened, and Matron was standing smiling.

"Come in, Mabel," she said, "would you like some tea?"

"Yes, please, Matron," said Mabel nervously, wondering what on earth was going on. Matron poured two cups from a pot and passed one to Mabel, along with a sugar bowl and milk jug.

"Help yourself," she said as she took a seat, behind her large desk. "Make yourself comfortable," she said as she pointed to a guest chair. "You must be wondering why I've asked you here, Mabel?"

"Yes, Matron, I was a bit," said Mabel anxiously.

"Well. I've got quite a busy job, Mabel, and sometimes I need a bit of help to keep the offices clean and tidy, to make tea for guests and visitors, and to type up a few letters and memos."

"Oh, sorry, I don't know how to type, Matron," said Mabel.

"We don't need to worry about that yet, Mabel, you can learn," she said reassuringly.

"You will be Matron's assistant and you will come here Monday to Friday from 9.00 am to 3.00 pm. You will go back to the ward at 12.00 every day for your lunch and come back here at 12.45 pm." She went on to explain her cleaning duties, how she liked the rooms to look after cleaning and that she would inspect them every day to make sure she was doing them properly. She also showed Mabel how to do different trays of refreshments for different visitors and let her practice carrying a heavy tray. She then explained that she would be accompanying her on her rounds for a few days, so that she could find her way around the whole site as she may need to be sent on errands or to take mail or memos to different departments. She then showed her to a little corner of her large office where she had a small desk and chair with a typewriter and pens and ink.

"This will be your desk, Mabel," she said with a smile.

"Oh, Matron! Thank you!" she said. "My own desk!" She was over the moon to be shown such trust and assured Matron that she wouldn't let her down.

"If I have visitors, it may be confidential, so once you have made them a drink, you will have to leave the office until I tell you to come back in. You could do other things, like making sure the committee room is clean and tidy," she said.

"Yes, Matron, whatever you say," replied Mabel.

When she returned to E2 for her lunch, she could feel the curiosity of the staff, wondering what on earth Matron wanted from her. Eventually Sister Jeffries broke the silence and said, "Let's be having you then! What's the story?"

Mabel deliberately took her time answering as she could see their anxiety. "From today," said Mabel, "I am Matron's assistant. Her eyes and ears on the ground. I even have a desk and chair in her office."

"Holy fuck!" said Jeffries.

Mabel sat with the other patients and had some lunch. It felt quite settled for a change, everyone was present, and she couldn't smell Paraldehyde which was always a good sign. She sat with Theresa and Margaret and whispered to them that they could relax and stop worrying because she had a direct line to Matron and would report any mistreatment that she saw.

She was beginning to feel very powerful for a young girl, when Theresa said, "Be careful, Mabel, they have a way of getting rid of people who don't toe the line in this place."

"What do you mean, Theresa?" asked Mabel.

"Just be careful, that's all I'm saying. They'll wind you up and make you go crazy so that you're always in the seclusion room, knocked out, and they'll make up things about you when anyone asks where you are," said Theresa.

"Oh God," said Mabel, "I hadn't thought of that. You're right, I will have to be very careful."

Later that afternoon, when she got back from her first day in her new role, she was met with a barrage of sarcasm and insults from the staff. "Oh, here comes Matrons little lap dog."

"Murphy's been sucking up to Matron all day, tittle-tattling and telling tales."

She was managing to ignore most of it and was doing a good job of pretending it didn't hurt when Jeffries said, "You're a loony, just like your mum and you're never getting out of here!" Mabel erupted at the unwarranted attack on her mother and lunged at Sister Jeffries, punching her square in the face, knocking her backwards and grabbing her throat with both hands.

"Don't you ever mention my mother, you fucking old witch!" she screamed as she sat astride her and choked her tightly. She could see her colour change and a tinge of blue appearing in Sister's face and, at that moment, she felt something hit the side of her head and her body was dragged backwards and on to the floor where she was restrained by staff as she reoriented herself, after the blow to her head.

She was still struggling and screaming when Sister Jeffries leaned over, with blood pouring from her nose and mouth and said, "Here we go again, Mabel Murphy, assaulting a nurse, you really need to learn to control that temper."

Mabel was writhing under the weight of two nurses and shouted, "*You* can explain to Matron why her assistant was needled and locked-up, you stupid, nasty woman!" Her words were more powerful than she realised, and she saw doubt appear in the eyes of the staff.

"She won't believe a word you say, Murphy, you're nothing but a little liar and a whore," said Sister Jeffries.

"I may be all of those things, Sister Jeffries, but unlike you, she likes me!" said Mabel with a wide smile. She knew that her verbal blow had landed when Jeffries didn't respond.

"Let her up," she instructed the staff. "Now get to bed and don't let me see you again before I leave or God help me, I'll knock the shit out of you!" Mabel felt very emotionally strong in that moment and pranced towards the dormitory doors. "Good night, ladies!" she said with a beaming smile as she left the dayroom.

The stand-off between Mabel and staff continued as they were less likely to abuse patients knowing that she had such direct access to Matron. However, it happened in much more subtle ways such as her meals being made too salty for her to eat or her possessions disappearing. She had also written a few letters to her parents and wondered if they had ever been posted, so she had managed to sneak one out in Matron's mail and feared that they had replied but it was being withheld by staff. She was beginning to tire of always being alert and vigilant because she never knew how or when Jeffries mob would strike again. Although she felt generally safe, she knew that they were clever, opportunistic and she had to constantly be one step ahead of them.

A few weeks later, on a Wednesday afternoon, she was in Matron's office when a telephone call came in. She heard Matron say, "Oh really? I'll be right down." And she left the office. Mabel prepared a tray, thinking that someone must be arriving for a meeting, then she heard Matron coming back up the stairs and showing people into the committee room.

She assumed it must be more people, so was adding cups to the tray when Matron came in and said, "Mabel, do you have a minute?"

"Yes, Matron," she replied as she walked out to the landing. Matron opened the door to the committee room and there, sitting at the long table were her mum and dad.

"Mum! Dad!" she screamed and began to sob, running towards them and hugging them both.

"I'll leave you to it," said Matron and she closed the door. Her parents looked frail and worried, but she was so happy to see them after almost two years absence.

"Oh, Mabel," said her mum. "What have you got yourself into, my girl?"

Mabel quietened and looked at her mum. "I didn't do anything, Mum, I promise."

"Mabel," said her dad. "We know everything now, your assault on the Mother Superior and you seemingly just going wild. What's happened to you?"

"It's not how it sounds, Dad," said Mabel. "They were cruel and were treating me very badly."

"Enough, Mabel!" said her mum, who looked like maybe she had just had a spell in hospital herself. "We have tried to understand you and what you've done, but you were in the papers! All the neighbours now know about the baby as well as all the other stuff. We don't know what to do!"

At that point, Matron gently kicked the door open and put down the tray of tea which Mabel had prepared. "Help yourselves," she said before closing the door behind her. Mabel poured the teas and placed them in front of her mum and dad.

"Does that mean you're not taking me home?" asked Mabel through blinding tears. "We're not allowed to take you home," said her dad. "You're here indefinitely by order of the courts."

"What does that mean, Dad?" she asked.

"It means that only they can decide when you are no longer a risk and are safe to live outside again."

"But there's nothing wrong with me!" protested Mabel. "It's the nuns and the nurses who drove me to it, I swear!"

Her dad shook his head slowly and said, "Oh, Mabel, what have you become? My gentle little girl, now so angry and violent, I can't believe this situation. Locked up in an Asylum…"

His words tapered off and Mabel said, "You both sent me away, what could I do? I was being treated badly, they took my baby away and then beat me when I was upset. I had to fight to survive."

Her mum was sobbing quietly and said, "I'm so sorry, Mabel, this is all my fault. If I had been stronger, you wouldn't have got close with that boy, Tom."

"It wasn't that boy Tom!" shouted Mabel. "It was Father Cullen when you were in bed sick!" She felt her body react at the thought of him touching her.

"Mabel!" said her father. "I won't hear this terrible accusation against a man of God!"

"But it's true!" said Mabel. "He's not a man of God, he's a monster! And so is Mother Superior! Cruel and evil!" She could see the tears in her father's eyes, and she could feel his disappointment in her. "Why won't you believe me?" she pleaded. "I'm a good girl!"

"I can't do this if you continue to say these things, Mabel," said her dad. "Father Cullen has been very good to us over the years and to a lot of other families I might add. You can't just make up stuff like that about a man of the cloth. Maybe it's best we just go."

"Please don't go, Dad, I'm sorry to upset you, but I'm telling the truth and nobody believes me."

Her mum, Betty, was quiet but had a strange expression on her face. "You believe me, don't you, Mum?" Mabel asked desperately.

"I'm not saying I believe the Father Cullen story, but I've been in and out of Claybury many times over the years, and I've seen some terrible things happen," she said. "Sometimes I was glad of the drugs as I didn't have to think about it when I was half-asleep, but it was very hard when I knew bad things were happening."

The tears were flowing as Mabel looked at her dad and said, "See, Dad, even Mum knows!"

"Put your coat on, Betty, we're going," said George. "I just can't take this right now, from both of you! It's too much!"

"Please don't, Dad, stay a little longer," begged Mabel, but his mind was made up.

"Goodbye, Mabel," he said, followed by, "I'll see you downstairs, Betty." And he left the committee room.

Betty hugged Mabel, still crying, and said, "You be very careful, my girl. I'm sorry we've come to this situation but, time is a great healer and things will get better." Mabel felt grief-stricken as she saw her mum leave the room and head downstairs. She sat down and put her head on the table as she released her deep sorrow and anger.

Matron walked in and quietly said, "Oh, Mabel, are you alright?" but she couldn't answer. Matron stood next to her and patted her back, uncomfortable with the emotions. "It will be alright, Mabel," she whispered. "You'll be alright."

9

As the months rolled forward, Mabel became more and more comfortable in her surroundings. She began to understand the system and had become very good at manipulating situations to her benefit rather than fighting everyone who didn't treat her well. She learned how to act humbly and say thank-you, much of it learned it has to be said, by working in Matrons' office. She was privy to a lot of conversations, some of them very important, and had learned from her Grandmother Beryl, that keeping a confidence was very important in maintaining any trust within a relationship, so she tried to ensure that she stuck to that rule. She had also made a few new friends across the hospital, including an older man called Jimmy who was a long-term patient on the male side.

Every week they held a dance in the recreation hall where the nurses would supervise the proceedings to make sure there were no sexual shenanigans going on. That's where she met Jimmy who had been in the Great War and had been 'shell-shocked' in battle. It meant that a lot of the time he was pretty normal, but sometimes, if there were loud noises or lots of people around him, he could become confused, start screaming and would lash out at people. In the dance, he sat away from the main crowd in the corner and if it got too noisy for him, he could slip out to the foyer until he settled down again. Mabel had seen him doing this a few times and that's how they began chatting, as she followed him out one evening to check he was alright.

He reminded her of her own dad and if she was upset, he would say "Come here and give Jimmy a big cuddle," and he would hold her tight for a few moments, until nurses arrived and said, "None of that nonsense!" before making them separate. There was never anything sexual between Mabel and Jimmy, neither had even thought about it, and Mabel often thought that it was the nurses who had dirty minds, rather than the patients misbehaving.

Most of the population on both the male and female blocks now recognised Mabel as she was often with Matron on her rounds and had started to command some respect from her fellow inmates. She was always smartly dressed and well behaved and she would chat to them whilst Matron was in the offices meeting with the Sister of Staff Nurses. She enjoyed feeling quite 'important' and more like a member of staff than one of the patients. It made her feel less ashamed of her past and why she was there. She had also learned how to type letters, albeit slowly and sometimes clumsily, particularly if the ribbon needed changing when she could be covered in ink and tied up in knots trying to fit everything back together. Matron was generally very patient and supportive with her, but occasionally would shout at her if things were taking too long or if someone was putting pressure on her.

"Just get it bloody-well done, Mabel, for God's sake!" she would scream, which would really upset Mabel as she loved and relied on Matron and would do anything to please her.

Fortunately, it was usually short-lived and soon afterwards she would say, "I'm sorry for shouting, Mabel, I'm under a lot of pressure and I don't mean to take it out on you." This made everything melt away and Mabel would once again be happy.

On her own ward, E2, Mabel still had to navigate the hostile actions of Sister Jeffries most days. Sometimes it was quite blatant, abusive behaviour, usually when there were no witnesses, such as name-calling or physical tormenting, poking or little slaps on the back of the head, hoping that she would lose control and attack someone.

Despite her position of trust, it still occasionally happened, particularly if her menstrual cycle was approaching, and she would be restrained, jabbed and locked up for a few days, but not before she had landed a few punches on the perpetrators. This would also involve a period of not working following an incident, usually around 14 days, but sometimes she felt it was worth it, when she saw the bad nurses with black eyes and bruises which she had given them. Matron was very forgiving and was aware that some of the nurses were 'heavy handed' in their approach, but there were serious shortages of staff across the whole establishment, and she couldn't afford to lose any, even if they were bad at their jobs.

It was at one of the dances that she met another girl called Faith who had been living in F1, which was a more secure ward, with locks on all the doors and bars on the windows. They got chatting and, despite Faith being quite loud and aggressive, Mabel liked her and found her very funny. She smoked like a trooper and had opinions about everyone and everything, but she was very pretty and had a fantastic laugh.

"Have you got that old cow Jeffries in your ward?" she asked.

"Oh, yes!" said Mabel.

"Give her a hard smack on the mouth from me, will you?" said Faith with a laugh.

"I'm due a run-in with her soon so I'll let you know when it's done!" Mabel laughed.

"I've got a good idea, Mabel," said Faith. "Next week, when we're meant to be here, why don't we climb the wall and head to the dance in town? We could get a couple of boyfriends who ain't off their rockers and have some fun!"

"Are you serious?" asked Mabel.

"'Course I am!" said Faith. "I've done it before! I got drunk on sweet sherry and stayed with one of the boys, in his dad's shed! We were at-it all night!" She threw her head back laughing at the memory. "Stick with me, Mabel, you might actually have some fun!"

Mabel thought of Tom and how much she liked him, but they hadn't even really kissed, and here was Faith talking about 'doing it' with strangers. She felt guilty just thinking about it, but also found the thought of the adventure very exciting.

"Next week," said Faith, "I'll meet you here at 7.00 pm, and when the nurses go into the kitchen for a cuppa, we can be over the wall behind the Nurses Home and into town before they finish their tea!"

"Oh, I'm not sure," said Mabel nervously. "I don't want to get into trouble."

"What trouble, Mabel! A couple of days in seclusion? Piece of cake!" said Faith persuasively.

Mabel weighed up the pros and cons for a few moments, then looked at Faith and said, "Let's do it!"

For the whole week, Mabel had trouble concentrating as she was so excited and yet, terrified at what she was planning to do. On the Saturday, she made sure her best dress was clean. It was an ugly, hospital issue, pinafore-dress, but she secretly unpicked some of the seams and made it look a bit more fitted with some neat stitching. She wore a coat on top to avoid suspicion and headed to the rec-hall. At first, she couldn't see anyone from F1, then she saw them arriving and sitting down at some empty tables whilst the nurses served them teas. She saw Faith discreetly look at her and give a 'thumbs up' sign, then the nurses headed for the kitchen to make their own tea. They never drank the same tea as the patients! As soon as the last nurse entered the kitchen, Faith signalled and they both headed out to the foyer to begin their escape.

They ran across the grassy area to the Nurses Home which was a large building over several floors. "This way!" said Faith as she ran down the side of the building and turned right at the end where they could then see the large wall which surrounded the asylum. "Quick! Climb up!" said Faith. "There are some ridges in the stone where you can get a good grip with your feet."

Mabel followed Faith's movements and was soon sitting on top of the wall looking out to the road and some little houses opposite. "Right, climb down and hang on with your hands then let yourself drop to the ground," said Faith knowingly, and Mabel followed her instructions. They both landed on the ground and brushed themselves down with their hands to get rid of any dirt or moss from the climb. They took one look at each other and burst out laughing with the fear and excitement. "Follow me!" said Faith as she crossed the road and ran along a footpath between the houses, and there, a few hundred yards away, was the village hall.

They could hear the orchestra music as they approached and Faith said to Mabel, "Watch, and do what I do." There were two gentlemen sitting at a small table busily taking admission fees from the queue, but Faith walked behind the queue and went straight into the ladies, followed closely by Mabel. "Right," said Faith. "Now we take out coats off and carry them over one arm, straight into the hall as if we've already been in."

Mabel followed the instructions carefully and very soon; they were both sitting at a small table near the stage. "Oh my God, we did it, Faith!" said Mabel. "I can't believe we're here!"

"Take it easy, Mabel," said Faith. "We ain't quite home and dry yet!"

"What do you mean?" asked Mabel.

"Watch and learn," said Faith as she approached the bar area looking very coy. Before she had reached the bar, Mabel saw a young man approach her and start chatting, then Faith pointed to where Mabel was sitting and then she saw Faith walking back on her own. "Bingo!" she said as she arrived back at the table. "Two sweet sherries on their way over, with two handsome blokes!"

"You're terrible!" said Mabel, laughing nervously.

"I know!" said Faith. "That's why I'm locked up with you!" And they both laughed.

Ralph and Bob were two local 18-year-old lads, both working as builder's labourers on some new housing which was going up over Coulsdon way, although Ralph said he was going to university later in the year. They were both single and were each looking for a nice girl to settle down with, but they were also happy to have a little fun along the way.

As they sat drinking and chatting with Mabel and Faith, it looked like they had known each other for years and you would never have thought that the two girls were escapees from the asylum. The chit chat, laughter and dancing were non-stop, and Mabel suddenly realised from the wall clock that it was almost 10.00 pm.

She grabbed Faith's arm and whispered loudly, "It's almost ten, Faith, we have to get back!"

"Ah fuck 'em!" said Faith. "We're as well, being hung for a sheep as a lamb! I'm staying!"

Mabel thought about the consequences and had to agree, that the punishment would be similar for either offence, so she smiled and said, "You're right, Faith, fuck it!" And they continued to laugh and dance the night away.

As everything began to close down and they were putting their coats back on to leave, Ralph said, "Does anyone fancy a night-cap at my house? My parents are in London visiting my grandparents, so I have the house to myself until Monday!"

Without discussion or even a glance, Faith said, "Yes, please!" and jumped up and down excitedly.

Mabel looked at her sheepishly and said, "Faith, I'm not sure about, you know, being with a man in that way. I'm scared."

"You'll be fine, Mabel. You've had a baby before, haven't you? You know what it's about? As they say, just lie back and think of England. Oh, and make sure he pulls out or you'll have another baby!" she said humorously.

Mabel temporarily fell silent, but once again 'sheep or a lamb' came into her consciousness and she reconnected with the group. After about a ten-minute walk, they arrived in a beautiful tree-lined street with a road-sign which said 'Lacey Avenue'. Mabel was open-mouthed at the size and grandeur of the houses. "They're not connected to each other!" she said. "And look at these huge gates and gardens, and cars! People here have got cars!"

"What does your dad do?" asked Faith. "You must be loaded to live here!"

"He's a Bank Manager," said Ralph, "and Mum has a little dress shop in town."

"Very nice!" said Faith. "I'm needing a new dress actually!"

He turned the key and opened the door, and, for Mabel, it felt like walking into a palace, with beautiful chandelier lights, deep carpets everywhere, dark shining wood and amazing French polished furniture. "Wow!" said Mabel as she slowly rotated so that she could take everything in. "This house is the poshest I've ever seen!"

"Oh yeah?" said Ralph. "You been in many posh houses then?"

"No, but I've seen them in pictures," said Mabel, quietly remembering but unable to share the beauty of the Convent Building.

"Right! Who's for a drink?" asked Ralph. "Scotch, Gin, sherry?" As Ralph poured the drinks, Bob opened up the gramophone and started to play a '78' record of a dance band. They pushed back the two large red velvet chesterfield sofas and rolled-up a Persian rug before they started dancing in couples, Mabel with Ralph and Faith with Bob.

"Is this a waltz?" asked Mabel, clueless as to what she was doing.

"No!" said Faith. "A waltz is, one-two-three, one-two-three. This is a foxtrot!" Mabel was still none the wiser and simply tried to follow Ralph's feet. After a few drinks and feeling quite tipsy, both couples began kissing passionately and gradually crept upstairs to their appointed bedrooms where, for Mabel at least, a night of passionate and exciting love-making took place and she felt happier than she had felt in years.

As the light shone through a gap in the heavy curtains, Mabel realised it was morning and time to go back to her reality. She rolled over to discover Ralph was not in the bed with her, but she could smell food and could hear him chatting to Bob downstairs. Just then, the door opened and in walked Faith wearing a bath robe. "Well, Mabel? How was it?" she asked, with a devious smile.

"Oh, Faith, I had the most amazing time, but the Police will be looking for us now so we'd better head back!" whispered Mabel, beginning to panic.

"We'll head back after breakfast," said Faith confidently. "We can tell them we will meet them next week but, whatever happens, they can't find out we're inmates in the asylum!"

"Oh, what are we going to do, Faith? We're in so much trouble!" said Mabel as they both started laughing out loud.

"Sounds like you two are awake! Breakfast is ready!" called Ralph from downstairs.

"Won't be long!" called Mabel as they both ran around trying to get dressed and look presentable. They sat downstairs and had a full breakfast of sausages and eggs with tea, and it was everything that Mabel could have wanted. She looked around the room and loved every single thing she could see, from the hand-printed wallpapers to the China cups and saucers and the white linen tablecloth.

"Penny for your thoughts?" said Ralph.

"Oh, I'm just daydreaming, don't mind me!" she said with a sigh.

"We have to go somewhere straight after this," said Ralph, "is there somewhere I could drop you?"

Mabel looked at Faith and they both began to panic. "Could you drop us at the road just by the village hall please? I can call my cousin to pick us up from there if that's suitable."

"No problem at all, let's be having you then!" said Ralph as he threw the dishes into the sink.

"We can wash them," said Mabel.

"No need," said Ralph, "we have a maid in the afternoons."

"How the bleedin' other half live!" said Faith.

As they got into the back seat, Mabel whispered to Faith, "The road by the village hall? Your cousin? What the hell's going on?"

Faith burst out laughing and said, "Go with the flow, Mabel, trust me, I've done this before!" They got out of the car and leaned in to kiss their escorts goodbye.

"When will I see you?" Ralph asked, as Mabel stood up.

"Maybe next week at the dance," she replied. "We'll see." And she gave a smile and a little wave as the car pulled away.
"Fuck me, we're in trouble!" said Faith with a huge grin.

"Dear God, I know!" said Mabel. As they entered the front gates, they could see the gate-lodge porter picking up the telephone to notify the wards that they were back.

"In here, you two, and don't move a muscle! We've had police out looking for you all night!" They sat in the gate-lodge office until they heard the sound of several people running towards them. Four female and two male nurses ran into the room and grabbed each of them, putting arm restraints on them, fastened from behind. They were then frogmarched to their respective wards and delivered safely inside, still restrained from behind.

"Well, well, well," said Sister Jeffries. "What do we have here? Is it a little runaway whore? Is it a woman of the night who's been out making a few shillings to feed her family? Or is it Matron's little helper who's finally shown that she's nothing but a filthy guttersnipe!" At that point she spun like a discus-thrower, and smacked Mabel hard across the face, knocking her off her chair and on to the floor. "I owed you that one, missy!" she said as she dragged her back up into the chair, in front of the onlooking staff and inmates. "Now, where have you been and who have you been with?" she demanded.

"I've been nowhere, Sister. We went out for a walk and got lost," said Mabel unconvincingly.

"You went out for a walk? But first you climbed a six-foot wall! What do you take me for?" she shrieked, but Mabel wasn't for escalating the situation as her hands were tied behind her back and she couldn't defend herself. She kept her cool, which was the last thing Jeffries wanted. "I hope you were careful, or you'll be back in that mother and baby unit pretty damned sharpish!" said Jeffries, still intent on baiting her whilst she couldn't defend herself.

"Take these restraints off and I'll show you what a guttersnipe I can be," said Mabel, in an attempt to make her back down. "I'm gonna get secluded anyway, so I'd be as well beating the shit out of you to make it worth it."

Sister Jeffries was becoming unsettled with the threats Mabel was making and changed her approach. "We got off on the wrong foot, Mabel, maybe we need to draw a line in the sand and start again." she said in an apologetic tone.

"We didn't get off on the wrong foot, Sister, you got off on the wrong foot!" said Mabel. "You are a nasty, cowardly bully and you just love to hurt people who are weaker than you. But I'm stronger than you, and you know it! That's why you hate me so much, because you're frightened of me!" At that point a small ripple of applauds could be heard along with some laughter and cheering amongst the patient population. Mabel could see the fine beads of sweat appearing on Jeffries' upper lip and her body language was becoming more and more uncomfortable.

"Why don't we call a truce and try to be kinder to each other?" suggested Jeffries.

"What about everyone else? You going to stop bullying them too?" asked Mabel.

"This is about you," said Jeffries, "I'm not interested in anyone else."

"See, that's the difference between me and you, Sister," replied Mabel. "I DO care about the others and I'm going to stand up for them whenever I feel it's needed." And again, there was some cheering and clapping from the patients.

"What is it about you, Murphy, that makes you think you're better than everyone else?"

"Probably the same thing that makes you think it's acceptable to attack and hurt people who are weaker than you," said Mabel. "I don't know what it is, but I'd rather be me than you."

Mabel could see how much this last statement had hurt Jeffries and, for a moment, she saw the fearful girl beneath the uniform and, for the first time, she felt pity for her. "Let's see how things go," suggested Mabel and Sister Jeffries nodded her head in agreement.

"I still have to put you in seclusion," she said.

"I know, but you don't have to kill me first," said Mabel with a knowing smile. Jeffries undid her restraints and they walked together to the seclusion room with no aggression or violence whatsoever. "See how much easier that was?" joked Mabel. Jeffries actually broke into a smile and nodded her head.

"Get undressed, I'll get you some food," she said as she slammed the door and locked it. Mabel got into the cotton nightdress and sat on the hard bed, wondering why things felt like they were changing. She had spent a wonderful evening with normal human beings and loved it. Nobody knew she was an inmate, and she felt the same as everyone else. Now Sister Jeffries was being nice to her which was actually scarier than anything else.

A short time later some food arrived, and Sister Jeffries said, "You know you need to do 24 hours in here, but, provided you're no trouble, I'll let you out when I come in tomorrow."

"Thank you, Sister," said Mabel, in the most trusting way she had ever responded to this woman. Mabel hoped that, just maybe, things were really changing and she could start looking forward to the future.

8.00 am sharp the next morning, Mabel heard the key turn in her room and there stood Sister Jeffries. "Good morning," she said very quietly.

"Good morning, Sister," replied Mabel.

"Don't worry, I'm keeping my word, but I have some bad news for you and it depends how you handle the news, whether or not I let you out," said Sister Jeffries cautiously.

"Is it my mum or dad?" Mabel panicked.

"No, Mabel, it's not your parents. Calm down," she replied. "It's your friend Faith Green from F1."

"Oh God, what's happened? Has she run away again, Sister? What's wrong?" pleaded Mabel.

"Sit down, Mabel, and I'll tell you," she said quietly. "When Faith got back to F1 yesterday, she kicked-off big time and knocked out three nurses who were trying to sedate her, so they called in the male staff as backup. Anyway, you know what she's like, she fought like a tiger and eventually four of them were able to restrain her, but it took all of their weight and strength to hold her, and when they went to give the injection, she had died under them."

Mabel let out a scream at the top of her lungs which made Sister Jeffries jump, but it was a brief response and she fell to the floor crying for her first real friend since Sarah back in Leyton. Sister Jeffries was very supportive and hugged her as she sobbed, even fighting back some tears herself as, ironically, she had a quiet admiration for the ones who fought back. "They think her heart stopped 'cos she wasn't getting enough air," she said, trying not to state the obvious and not apportioning blame to anyone.

The atmosphere in E2 was very sombre, but very respectful and Sister Jeffries put her arm around Mabel and escorted her out of seclusion and back into the main ward where she could be with her friends and get the support she needed. As she sat in an armchair in the dayroom, beginning to compose herself, sister Jeffries crouched down beside her and said, "I'm so sorry, Mabel, for everything. If you need anything at all, just ask." And she gently squeezed her hand.

"Thank you, Sister, and I really mean that," said Mabel through her tears, before being invaded by a queue of inmates wishing to give their condolences.

It was later in the day that Mabel overheard Sister Jeffries chatting with the other nurses in the office and she said, "From now on, I don't want no trouble on my shift. I want to treat people better and not to feel so fucking shitty all the time. What happened yesterday on F1 could easily happen here and I'm done with it! I've enough guilt on my conscience as it is without adding someone's life to it!"

Mabel felt something release inside when she heard this, as if Faith's death could maybe make a difference and make people change their ways. She felt hope, gently returning to her heart and said a few prayers for Faith, wishing that she had finally found happiness and peace. "No more fighting, my friend, rest in peace," she said as she made the sign of the cross for the first time since she left the convent.

The coming weeks and months were, in the main, very pleasant and, apart from the occasional momentary loss of control, Sister Jeffries was a different person. She even began to share information about herself and her own difficult upbringing which had led her to becoming a nurse. She also had a disabled adult at home who needed a lot of care, so her life was tough and relentless. Mabel was adamant that this did not excuse her previous cruelty in any way, but she felt it went some way to explain why someone could be so angry, so much of the time.

Although they had a very different relationship now, Mabel never took it for granted and knew that Sister Jeffries may have the capacity to switch back to her old self without too much trouble, although she hoped and prayed that she was mistaken, however, as months became years, she began to forget how Sister was and accepted that she had made a huge effort and had managed to change into a better person. Mabel was beginning to understand the concept of forgiveness and started to think about the other people who did her wrong, such as Father Cullen, Mother Superior, or even her parents. She found that she felt better and happier when she didn't dwell on the bad stuff as it made her angry and self-piteous, so she started trying to let go of the anger she felt, which was not an easy feat.

Her job with Matron was also going well and she had been allowed out with staff to buy some smart clothes for her work, as her confidence was growing and Matron was beginning to really rely on her, so Mabel had developed a strong sense of purpose and her self-confidence had grown considerably. When she looked in the mirror, she saw a smart and attractive woman looking back at her, which was a very new experience.

10

It was now late 1940 and the Second World War was in full swing across Europe and was affecting many people. Most of the young men from around the country had been conscripted and were off fighting in the Army, Navy and Air Force. Munitions and fire-arms factories had been set up and lots of women were now working full-time, doing very tough jobs which were regarded 'men's work' as well as bringing up children. This included the Asylum, who turned the recreation hall into a makeshift 'production line' manned by inmates who were trained to perform various jobs such as, filling kit-bags with gas-masks or other items needed by soldiers. They also packed lots of boxes with supplies and sealed them shut, for collection by the military, usually the Coldstream Guards who were based in Caterham.

There was also a 'blackout' every night so that German planes could not identify populated areas and drop bombs as they had started to do around London, so new routines were introduced which included all windows being covered by heavy blackout curtains every evening until the next morning. There were air-raid wardens who spent their evenings knocking on any doors where they could see light coming through and imposing fines if they didn't rectify it.

The Asylum continued to run like clockwork, largely unaffected apart from the occupational situation in the hall, and the loss of a few male nurses who had volunteered to fight rather than stay in a reserved job which was exempt from being 'called-up' Things were tough in other areas though, such as food supplies, although the asylum had a huge area which inmates farmed and grew lots of vegetables, but they had to start sharing their crops with the local villages as well as needing security to prevent theft of the crops. People could often be seen stealing potatoes or cabbage, filling canvas sacks and running like the wind before they could be caught.

Mabel, now 24, was still working with Matron and had some real authority around the asylum, commanding love and respect from most of the population. She had tried for release several times and had been up in front of the Hospital Board, but because of the severity of her assault on the nun and, on paper at least, she had a history of violence and absconding since being committed, therefore she was never granted her freedom. She got the occasional 'Day-Pass' on a Saturday when she could go out of the hospital unescorted, so long as she was back by 5.00 pm. If she was late without a good reason, her pass would be rescinded, and she would have to go through the whole application process again.

Her dad stayed in touch with the occasional letter but, reading between the lines, he didn't seem to be coping too well and it seemed her mother Betty was now a long-term Claybury inmate, which made Mabel very sad as she still missed them terribly. It took a long time for her to accept that she wasn't going back home and that she had to look at her long-term future from within the walls of the Asylum, even though she knew that there was nothing wrong with her. She was trapped by the system and by the punishing attitude of the courts, towards women who made mistakes. Men seemed to be able to do whatever the hell they liked, but not women. They were punished severely and made to carry the guilt and shame for others, including violent husbands who treated them like property. If she allowed herself, Mabel could become very angry at the injustices in her world, not just those visited on her, but those visited on most of the people she lived with.

It was during one of her day-passes that, just for the fun of it, she took the bus to Godstone, and was walking down the high street looking in shop windows, when she realised that someone was staring at her, a handsome young man of about 25 years, smiling directly at her. She looked over her shoulders to make sure he wasn't smiling at someone else and smiled back. He crossed the street towards her, reached out his hand and said, "Hello, I'm Archie, nice to meet you."

Mabel responded by shaking his hand and said, "Mabel, nice to meet you too."

"Do you fancy a cup of tea?" asked Archie. "There's a little tea-room down the street."

"That would be lovely, thank you, Archie," said Mabel and they walked the few yards together and found a seat in the tearoom. "Tea for two please," said Archie.

"Would you like something to eat?" he asked Mabel.

"No thanks," she replied, "tea is fine."

They chatted very politely whilst the waitress arrived and laid their dishes and teapots on the table, then Mabel piped-up and bravely said, "How come you've not been called up then?"

Archie looked slightly taken aback and said, "Cor blimey, that didn't take long, girl!"

Mabel apologised. "Sorry, I didn't mean to be rude, it's just so strange to see a young lad not in uniform," she said.

"Don't worry, I'm not a conscientious objector!" he said with a smile. "I have a condition called epilepsy, so I sometimes have fits and when I went to sign-up, they couldn't take me. I feel a bit bad about it but there's not a lot I can do."

"Oh, Archie, I didn't mean to pry and I'm sorry you've got epilepsy, it must be scary," said Mabel who had seen a few people have fits back in the Asylum but, unsurprisingly didn't share that information.

"Well. It's not so bad really, more embarrassing than anything else cos it always seems to happen in bleedin' public!" said Archie, trying to make light of his condition.

"Do you have fits often then?" asked Mabel.

"Well, about one every four to six weeks really, sometimes longer," said Archie. "I take a tablet called Phenobarbitone which stops them happening so often, although it sometimes makes me really sleepy."

"I'm glad it's not too serious and thank goodness you weren't sent abroad to fight, you could be killed if you had a fit during a battle!" said Mabel, trying to show some empathy and understanding. Now that she was sitting close-up, she could see some old scars and bumps around his head and mouth.

"They're from having fits," he said self-consciously as he saw Mabel staring. "I fall to the ground if I don't get a warning and usually do myself an injury, although I'm getting pretty good at sensing when one is coming, and I lie on my bed."

"Sounds like you've got it all under control," said Mabel, beginning to admire the young man opposite.

"What do you do?" asked Archie as he poured another cup of tea.

"I'm a nurse," said Mabel. "I work over in the Asylum."

"Wow!" said Archie. "That place looks scary!"

"It is at first, but you get used to it," said Mabel, quite enjoying the game she was playing and the fact that she didn't have to try and hide her connection to the place.

"Are there any really crazy people in there?" asked Archie curiously.

"Not really, Archie," said Mabel. "They've all got a story to tell and, once you understand that, they don't seem crazy anymore."

"Oh, you must be a fantastic nurse, Mabel," said Archie, "so caring and understanding."

"Well, I'm no different to anyone else really, just trying my best to get by," said Mabel humbly, before looking at her watch and saying, "Oh God, it's 4.15, I'd better get back!"

Archie paid the bill and walked Mabel back to the bus stop. "There should be one in a few minutes," said Archie. "When are you coming back this way? Can we do tea again?"

"I'm not sure of my shifts, Archie, but I could try and get here next week."

"Fantastic!" said Archie. "If you can make it, I'll meet you at the bust stop opposite at 1.00 pm, and if you don't show, I'll know you're working," he said as she got on the bus and, as it pulled away slowly, she waved from her seat.

When she got back to E2, Sister Jeffries called her into the office and sat her down. I had a telephone call just after you left, from Claybury Asylum. "Oh my God, Mum!" said Mabel.

"No, it's not your mum, I'm afraid it's your dad. He was found at home last week, sitting at the kitchen table. Probably a heart attack they reckon. Anyway, he was your mum's next of kin, so Claybury had to update their records which meant tracing you. Your mum is not in a good way I'm afraid, Mabel, so I'm trying to get permission for you to go up London for the funeral and maybe you could pop in and see your old mum as well."

"Thank you, Sister," said Mabel tearfully.

"How would you feel if I asked to go with you, for a bit of support?"

"Oh, that would be great," said Mabel.

"We'd have to do it all in one day, but I'll speak to Matron and see if we can be driven in the official car, that way we can go wherever we need to and not be relying on trains and buses."

Mabel sobbed quietly and said, "Thanks for being so kind, Sister, I won't forget this."

"No problem," said the woman who was once so terrifying. "We make a good team you and me!"

A few days later, the official car drove them first to Claybury Asylum in Chigwell. When they arrived, Sister Jeffries showed her badge and they were allowed through the gates and into the main buildings. On the ward, they were both shown to a screened-off bed, within a large dormitory. There in the bed lay Betty, mumbling nonsense, with saliva dripping from her mouth and both hands with very marked tremors.

"Mum," said Mabel as she gently shook her mum's shoulder. "It's me, Mabel."

Betty started to rock from side to side repeating, "Mabel, Mabel, Mabel, Mabel," over and over again, but not being aware of her surroundings. Her tongue seemed swollen and was making it difficult for her to talk, as if it was getting in the way. Mabel sat down on the bed beside her and took her hand, and the tremors were so strong that she could feel them vibrating up her arm.

"What on earth is wrong with her, Sister?" she asked as she watched this woman she loved, behave so strangely.

"Let me have a word with the Ward, Sister, and I'll find out for you," said Sister Jeffries and she disappeared to the small office with glass windows in the dayroom. Mabel was shocked at how thin and undernourished her mother appeared, her hands and arms were very bony and frail looking, but mostly it was her mental state which concerned her.

"Mum, can you hear me?" she asked.

But Betty just continued to babble, "Mabel, Mabel, bel, bel, bel, bel," as her mouth moved in chewing motions continuously.

Sister Jeffries re-appeared and said, "I've spoken to Sister and this apparently started with a bit of a stroke a few weeks back, she couldn't speak at all for a little while and then she was very distressed, so they had to sedate her with some very strong drugs and that's what causes some of the problems with her mouth. They also think the stroke may have triggered the onset of some sort of senile dementia, so they don't think she will get any better. They are talking about moving her to one of the ground-floor wards where she can be looked after in bed until she is ready to go."

"You mean die?" exclaimed Mabel.

"I'm afraid so," said Sister, "she's not taking any nourishment at all, so it's only a matter of time."

"Oh God," cried Mabel, "I can't cope with this! I'm here to bury my dad and my mum is going as well!"

Sister Jeffries hugged her and said, "You are one of the strongest women I know, Mabel Murphy. You have inspired me, and I know that you can get through this difficult time. I'm right here, by your side, for as long as it takes." Mabel heard the words and began to settle and gain her composure again.

She said a very quiet thank you as she squeezed Sister Jeffries' arm and sat back down on the bed.

"Mum, I've got to go and say goodbye to Dad, and I don't think I'll make it back for a little while, but I love you so much and am thinking of you every day," she said as she kissed her forehead.

Betty suddenly grabbed her arm, looked into her eyes and said, "Babababababababyebyebyebye……" before she drifted and returned to rocking from side to side.

"Did you see that, Sister?" said Mabel.

"I sure did, Mabel! She seemed to know it was you girl," said Sister Jeffries as they left the ward, arm in arm and returned to the waiting car.

They arrived outside St Johns Church in Leytonstone and both stepped out to see a waiting group of Mourners standing in a line. There, at the front of the group, was her nan, Beryl, looking very thin and unsteady, dressed in black, with a walnut walking stick. "Nan!" called Mabel and they both held each other tightly.

"Oh, my darling girl, I've missed you so much!" said Beryl through reluctant tears, Mabel just lost control and buried herself in her Nan's loving arms and sobbed. She then felt a gentle tap on her shoulder and when she turned around, there was her childhood friend, Sarah.

"Hello, Mabel," she said with a sad smile.

"Sarah!" said Mabel and again began sobbing. "Sorry, everyone," said Mabel, composing herself again, "This is Sister Jeffries, my friend."

"Call me, Marjorie," she said as she shook their hands. "You've got quite a granddaughter, Beryl," she said with a warm smile. The funeral was very basic, but the priest said some nice things about her father so Mabel was pleased.

She leaned in towards Beryl and said, "Thank you, Nan, that was beautiful," before she was pulled in closer and hugged tightly. They stood outside as the coffin left for the cemetery.

"Do we have to go too?" asked Mabel.

"No, darling, men only at the graveside so say your goodbyes now," said Beryl. She rushed up to the carriage, kissed her fingertips and touched the oak coffin.

"Bye, Dad, sorry I made you so unhappy, but I always loved you," she said as the carriage moved away from the front of the Church.

"There's a cuppa tea and a few sandwiches in the Church Hall if anyone would like to join us!" announced Beryl as she took Mabel's arm and headed to the hall door.

The four of them, Mabel, Sister Jeffries, Beryl and Sarah, were sitting at the main table and about twenty people, mostly old neighbours, had joined them for a very simple, funeral breakfast, consisting of a cup of tea, some meat-paste sandwiches and a scone with a little jam. They were catching up, chatting quietly, when Mabel felt goosebumps rising and the hair on the back of her neck started to bristle. She could feel her anxiety rise but didn't know why, then, out of the corner of her eye, she saw Father Cullen arrive and talk to one of the mourners.

Her body began to react and shake when Sister Jeffries noticed and said, "Whatever is wrong, Mabel, you look petrified and you're shaking!" Mabel couldn't speak as she tried to control her body and the trauma which was re-emerging. She felt sick, and ran out of the hall to the toilet, followed by Sister Jeffries.

"What on earth is wrong!" she asked.

Gradually, Mabel began to settle and said, "Father Cullen!"

"What about him?" quizzed Sister Jeffries.

"He raped me," she said, "and gave me the baby. That's how I ended up with the nuns."

Sister Jeffries stood up and shouted, "Bastard!" at the top of her lungs. "I remember now, you said something like that during one of our battles and I didn't believe you. God I'm so sorry, I can tell you are being honest. Look at the state of you!" she cried.

"I don't know what to do, Sister," said Mabel.

"Leave it to me," came the reply. "Go back to your seat and wait for me." They walked back into the hall together and Mabel discreetly pointed him out, before returning to her seat.

"Excuse me, Father Cullen, could we have a few words in private?" said Sister Jeffries.

"Do I know you, miss?" he asked.

"No, Father," she replied, but we have a mutual friend.

"Oh, I see," said the priest, "shall we pop out to the door for some privacy?"

"What a good idea," said Sister Jeffries. "Best no one hears this." Outside the door to the hall, Father Cullen leaned his back against the stone wall and lit a cigarette.

"What can I do for you," he asked.

"Well, Father," she said. "I'm a Nursing Sister in the South East London Asylum, where, for a number of years now, I've been looking after a very damaged and broken young girl."

"Oh, that sounds tragic," he interrupted, unaware that Mabel was only a few feet away in the hall.

"Yes, it is tragic, Father, for it was you who damaged and broke her!" she shouted as she grabbed his genitals with one hand and his throat with the other. "You dirty fucking abomination of a man!" she screamed whilst he writhed in agony at the twisting and crushing of his offending organ. "You have destroyed a young girl's life, not to mention the life of your own child who is, God knows where now! What a filthy, weak excuse for a man you are, Father, and I'm going to make sure you don't do it to anyone else!"

By now, he was breathless and begging for mercy, as several mourners had wandered out to see what the commotion was. "Get your fat, sweaty arse back in that hall, sit down and don't open your mouth or, God help me, I'll fucking kill you!" said Sister Jeffries.

He was shaking and panicking at the physical pain and humiliation he was feeling. Sister Jeffries walked behind him, gently pushing him to let him know she was there and wasn't going anywhere. She looked at the main table and saw Mabel and Beryl looking bemused at the distraught appearance of the priest. "Ladies and Gentleman!" she announced to the remaining mourners. "Father Cullen would like to say a few words, wouldn't you, Father!" and she pointed to an empty chair. "Sit!" she commanded, and he obeyed. The mourners were confused and intrigued. "Go on, Father! Say what you need to say!" demanded Sister Jeffries.

"It was all a big misunderstanding," he said quietly, through snot and tears. "How can it be a misunderstanding, Father, when you're an adult and you take advantage of a girl barely 14 years old!" replied the angry nurse. There was a rush of noisy energy through the room as the shock hit the small group of mourners. "This trusted, man of God, deliberately and viciously attacked a defenceless girl who was trying to take care of her sick mother. Not only that, but he left her with child, and stood back as she was castigated. He didn't lift a finger to help her or her family, in fact, he encouraged the lie that she had been having relations with a local boy."

Sister Jeffries then grabbed his clerical collar away from him and shouted, "Confess, Father! Isn't what I'm saying the truth?"

"Yes!" he cried. "Yes! Yes! I was weak and I am ashamed!" The mourners were in the early stages of becoming a lynch mob and were angrily shouting at him as he sat, shaking and weeping.

"I suggest someone let the Bishop know, as well as the police!" said Sister Jeffries as she approached the table where Mabel and the others sat. "Sorry, Mabel," she said, "I went back to me old self there for a minute."

Mabel stood up and hugged her tightly. "Thank you once again," she said. "And I don't mind the old you if you're defending me!" As they left the hall, Mabel approached Father Cullen and stood before him, but he could not look at her.

"Father, I wouldn't wish on you, what you have visited on me. I pray that you are punished for what you have done to me, and probably to countless others. I hope I never see or hear of you again as you have poisoned enough of my life already. For years, I thought it was me. I must have been bad, or I must have deserved it, but it wasn't me. It was you!" and she slowly backed away from him and joined the others who were leaving the hall.

"We best start to head back," said Sister Jeffries after having more tea and cake at Beryl's house.

"I'll try and get back up to see you, Nan," said Mabel.

"That would be lovely, darling," said Beryl with tears in her eyes, giving her a huge kiss. "Don't leave it too long, love, I'm getting on you know!" she said with a warm smile. They hugged at the front door and Mabel and Sister Jeffries got into the car for the journey back to the Asylum.

"That was quite a day, Mabel Murphy!" said Sister Jeffries, as the car turned into Leyton High Rd. "You did great!"

"Thanks, Sister," said Mabel, "and so did you! I can't believe that you got a confession out of Father Cullen!"

"I couldn't stop myself!" said Sister. "It happened to me too you know, and I just couldn't hold my anger when I knew he had done it to you!" They gently hugged in the back seat as they headed back to Surrey.

About two weeks later, Mabel got a letter from her Nan to say that the Police did not charge Father Cullen and that the Bishop had transferred him somewhere else out of London, which upset Mabel as she feared he would do the same thing to other children. She told Sister Jeffries and Matron and they shared her concerns, but said that, sadly, there was nothing which could be done if the Church were covering it up. The only possible option was to try and find out where he had gone and to let the parishioners know his history, but Matron added that, because he had no formal convictions, they may be breaking the law by slandering his name. They all agreed to let sleeping dogs lie and to hope and pray that he would not harm anyone else.

Six months later, Mabel received a letter from Sarah to say that her nan, Beryl, had passed away suddenly and was buried before she found out about it. When she asked them why no one had contacted Mabel, she was told that they didn't know where she was, so some other relatives buried her and broke up her house and possessions. Mabel was devastated by the news and became quite depressed for a time afterwards, not going to her job with Matron and just sitting in the dayroom, staring into mid-air. Eventually, she emerged from her grief-fog and slowly started to re-engage with everyone, particularly when she got a small package from Sarah, containing her nan's wedding ring, which one of her cousins had asked Sarah to give her. It was thin and worn, but it was her nan's and she treasured it.

11

It's September 1945 and the war is finally over, peace at last in Europe and the rest of the world. There were street parties all over England and the South East London Asylum was no exception. The staff and inmates had made miles of bunting and hung it all around the corridors and wards, there were tables of food and drinks outside and a local brass band played up-beat, celebration music. The atmosphere was wonderful because life could now go back to normal, so everyone celebrated, dancing and laughing with joy.

Mabel was manning a stall with Matron where they were serving tea and soft drinks to the patients and visiting family members. It was a bustling, busy stand and she wasn't paying attention to who was waiting to be served, when she heard "Hello stranger!" and there stood Archie whom she had met in Godstone several years before.

"Archie!" she exclaimed, happy to see him but remembering that she had told him she was a nurse.

"Do you never get a day off?" he asked.

Mabel looked at Matron and giggled. "Is it OK if I have a little break, Matron, I haven't seen Archie for a long time?"

"Go on!" said Matron. "You can have a lunch hour."

"Thank you," replied Mabel.

"Let's go for a walk," said Archie, "we've a lot of catching up to do." They got a couple of drinks and Mabel led him to an area where she often sat in the afternoons and early evenings, on a wooden bench beneath some beautiful trees. They chatted and laughed for what seemed like hours, and they had a really strong connection, so Mabel kept feeling guilty about the story she had spun him.

"Archie, there's something I need to tell you," she said.

"Oh yes," he replied.

"What's that then?"

"Remember when we met, and I told you I was a nurse?" asked Mabel.

"Yes, I remember," said Archie.

"Well, it wasn't exactly true," she went on. "When I was younger, I had a few problems in my life and, somehow, I eventually ended up here…as a patient!" She put her head down and looked at the floor, ashamed of the words she had just shared.

"Wow," said Archie. "I would never have guessed that in a million years! You're beautiful and clever and funny, I don't see any problems. I have epilepsy, now that's a problem!" he joked.

"I'm much better now," she reassured him. "I used to be very angry and stubborn, but I'm much quieter now." Archie lifted her head up from below her chin and smiled at her.

"I don't care about any of that stuff," he said. "Surely you can get out now?" he asked.

"Well, because I'm here by order of the court, they have to give permission for my release and, so far, they've refused," she said.

"On what grounds?" he asked.

"Well, it's a long story, but they think that I pose a threat."

"Oh God, that's awful, Mabel," he said.

"To be honest," said Mabel, "I've been here so long, I'd be frightened to move back outside. I know this place like my family, probably better than my family, and outside of these walls really scares me."

"In that case, I'll have to move in as a patient then." And they both laughed. Before returning to her stall duties, they agreed to meet up regularly when she had her day passes and, if he needed to get in touch, he could leave a note for her at the Admin Reception or the Gate Lodge where she would be able to pick it up.

Back at the stall, Matron was curious about Mabel's new suitor. "You're a dark horse, Mabel Murphy." She laughed. "Where have you been hiding him then?"

"Matron!" Giggled Mabel. "We met ages ago in Godstone and that's the first I've seen him since then."

"He seems a very nice young man, Mabel," said Matron. "Maybe once you get out of here, you two will get married." The thought of leaving the hospital filled her with terror, even though she really liked Archie. She had grown so accustomed to the routine and communal living that she feared she wouldn't cope on her own or only looking after one person. She had been there for so long that she forgot there was another life outside.

As the evening drew in, the patients started to return to their wards and the staff and visitors started to take down their stalls, Mabel was packing some boxes when Sister Jeffries appeared, dressed in her civilian clothes.

"Hello, Sister!" said Mabel. "I thought you were having some days off this week."

"I am, Mabel," she replied, "but I'm having a bit of a party with the family and neighbours tonight and I thought you might like to come."

"Are you serious?" said Mabel excitedly. "Well, I wouldn't be standing here if I wasn't, would I?" she replied.

"I've checked with Matron and she's given the all-clear."

"Fantastic!" said Mabel. "Let's go!" And they walked out to the gate where Sister Jeffries' husband was waiting in a small car to take them home to the party.

Sister Jeffries had a small, terraced house in a quaint, little street, a few miles from the Asylum. As they got out of the car, there were still some people celebrating in the street, singing and dancing to an electric gramophone which was sitting in someone's open window. As they walked into the house Mabel could hear the chatter and laughter coming from the sitting room and could see people standing around in the kitchen and hall. As they walked into the main room, everyone spontaneously began to applaud and Mabel joined them, looking around the room.

"They're clapping for you, Mabel!" said Sister Jeffries. "I've told them all about how much you've helped me, and they've all been dying to meet you!" Everyone started cheering for Mabel, and she was overwhelmed by the feelings.

"Oh, my goodness!" she managed to say, as the clapping continued.

Sister Jeffries signalled for them to settle down and said, "I'd just like to say a few words! I know today is all about peace returning and all that, but peace returned to my life a few years back when I met this young lady." And again, everyone started cheering. "We didn't hit it off to start with…No…I'll rephrase that…I didn't hit it off with her to start with, in fact I was a real cow! But this young girl taught me that I could be better than that, and all these people can bear witness to that. I've been a very different person these last few years and it's all down to you! I'd like everyone to raise a glass to Mabel Murphy!" she said.

And in one voice, the whole party raised their glasses and said, "Mabel Murphy!" and then started cheering and clapping again. Mabel felt the happiest and proudest she had ever felt, and for the first time she could remember, she was crying happy tears.

She threw her arms around Sister Jeffries and said, "Thank you so much, Sister!"

"Marjorie!" she replied. "We're not in work anymore."

Mabel had the most fantastic evening, meeting lots of new people, dancing and even singing a song on her own! The party went on until late and, when Mabel was dropped back at the hospital, she felt like she would never sleep with the feeling of excitement. She sat on her bed and looked at the rows of other patients snoring, and despite everything, she felt as if she was home. She lay down on her bed and listened to the familiar noises and groans, and smiled, because this is where she felt safe.

Although she disliked it at times, she had learned to be strong and to defend herself in this place, and she loved her extended family of patients, staff, and now, Marjorie's family and friends. She had a position with some status and authority, whereas, outside, she didn't feel confident as she had never had a 'real job' and was frightened of finding out that she wasn't good enough. She felt more fear outside the walls than inside, so this helped make up her mind that she would stay, at least until Matron retired!

A few weeks later, as she was polishing the wooden furniture in the committee room, Matron came in. "Mabel," she said. "Do you realise that you are now entitled to have your legal status reviewed again?"

"Yes, I do, Matron, but I feel I'm more needed here than out there, so I wasn't going to bother this time," she said.

"Oh," said Matron, "are you sure? There's a condition called Institutional Neurosis, which some people get if they've been in hospitals, prisons or asylums for too long. It makes them frightened of leaving and having to change the stable things in their lives. Maybe we could have a chat about it before you make any decisions."

"Yes, that would be great," said Mabel. "But I don't think that's me," she added.

That afternoon, they both sat down for a cup of tea and Matron said, "Mabel, I want you to think carefully before you make any decisions about your future. I know it seems a daunting task, moving out of here and taking responsibility for yourself, but you are a very clever and adaptable woman, and you could have a wonderful life outside of these gates. For the life of me, I don't know why they've kept you here for so long."

"Thank you for your kind words, Matron," she responded, "but I just feel that my purpose in life and the reason I wake up every day, is to be a strong support to you in your job, but also with and any other patients who need some support."

"You've certainly become an important person for many people, and not just patients I would add, but I'll be retiring in the next year, and I don't know who will replace me at this point. I hope that they would keep you on, but it may be someone with new and different ideas, so things may change anyway," said Matron. "I'm more institutionalised than anyone, and I'm worried about what I'm going to do without this place, so I have a good idea of how anxious and fearful you would be feeling."

"I'd at least like to stay until you retire and then see who comes in and, if there's no place for me, I'll maybe re-apply for release at that point. Is that a compromise you'd be happy with Matron?" she replied.

"Right, let's agree to review the situation within the next 12 months when we know how the land is going to lie as far as my successor goes," said Matron and they both smiled and pretended to do 'Cheers' with their teacups.

Back on E2 that evening, Mabel approached Sister Jeffries and said, "Did you know that Matron will be retiring in the next year?"

"Well, I knew it wasn't far-off, but didn't realise it was so close," she replied.

"Are you going to apply for her job?" asked Mabel curiously.

"Me? You're joking! I would never get it in a million years! My track record would be scrutinised and there would be others better suited than me," said Sister.

"Well, I disagree," said Mabel. "If you'd applied fifteen years ago, you wouldn't stand a chance." She laughed. "But you have been an amazing nurse and an all-round professional for a long time now. Don't hide your light under a bushel, as my nan Beryl used to say."

"Thanks, Mabel, but I'm a bit scared of the rejection if I didn't get it. Let's see how I feel nearer the time," she said.

“I can live with that!” replied Mabel. “And my important decisions can be made, once I know what is happening here.”

Ten months later, the Recreation Hall is decorated and packed with staff to celebrate Matron’s retirement. The Stage is set with table and chairs for some speeches, and the Hospital Director, Dr Melvyn Fotheringham is delivering the Farewell speech, thanking Matron for over 40 years’ service at the Asylum. He says lots of very nice things about her and there are lots of applauds and cheering when she received a gold carriage clock, followed by Matron’s closing words, where she thanked everyone for their kind words, and made a special mention of Mabel, for her years of dedication to supporting her in her role.

As the clapping and cheering continued, Matron said, “I would like to make one more announcement before I depart for the last time! I know there has been a lot of gossip and conjecture about my successor, so I would like to announce, that the new Matron of the South East London Asylum will be Marjorie Jeffries, and I would like to wish her many congratulations on securing the position and I hope she has as much happiness as I have had in the role.” The room went into uproarious celebrations, with all eyes turning on Sister Jeffries who, by this time, was crying with the shock. She was welcomed onto the stage and the table of dignitaries shook her hand and congratulated her for securing the position.

“Speech! Speech!” the audience chanted.

So she faced the crowd and said, “I would like to thank Matron and the Board for giving me the opportunity to take on this new and exciting role. I never believed that I would be successful, so that is why I am an absolute mess!” she said through her tears.

"I would also like to join Matron in thanking one very special person, who I believe has been instrumental in making me a better nurse and a much better person. Ladies and gentlemen, I give you Mabel Murphy!" The audience went wild whistling, cheering and clapping and Mabel was invited up onto the stage for some photographs which would go into the local papers the following week.

As the three of them stood together, facing the cheering crowd, Mabel leaned into them both and said, "Well, ladies, that's my decision made. I'm staying here for the time being."

Both of them smiled at her, especially the new Matron who laughed and said, "I'm gonna need you to teach me my new job!"

It was a day of emotional extremes for Mabel. Sadness at the loss of Matron who had taught, supported and protected her for many years now, giving her opportunities for personal growth which wouldn't necessarily have been available outside. And extreme joy, that her friend Marjorie would be filling that space and allowing her to continue with her own senior position within the hierarchy, which made her very happy.

12

It's now summer 1965 and lots of things have changed. The Asylums have been brought into the NHS and are now Hospitals and the South East London Asylum is now called Surrey Hills Regional Mental Hospital. Marjorie Jeffries is still Matron but lots of the rules and rituals within the hospital have changed, which initially Mabel had some real difficulty in accepting. The hospital was now open for most patients to go in and out as they pleased, except those who were in locked wards, but they now had to be held under sections of the Mental Health Act.

Mabel's status had also changed to 'Informal' so, technically, she could have left at any time, but she didn't want to go anywhere. In the interim, Matron Jeffries had allocated her a modified one-bed apartment, which was upstairs in the gate lodge. However, she only really slept there, as she was always actively in the middle of everything which was happening within the hospital.

It gave her a little bit more power and status within the hospital community, and she was generally looked upon by everyone as 'one of the staff' which she loved very much. She could often be seen, looking after patients who were upset or agitated or telling off patients who were being rude or aggressive to staff. She could manage even the most challenging patients with a strong look and a few words. She also had an absolutely astounding knowledge of the nurses' off-duty rotas and shift patterns.

She visited most wards, so she knew who was in, who was out, who was sick and who was on annual leave. Years of assisting Matron, made her a fount of knowledge regarding the staff situation and she loved being called upon and asked for favours by staff. Her hospital 'family' had made her feel valued and needed for most of her adult life, so she didn't miss what she didn't have as far as the outside world was concerned.

Archie had moved away and got married a few years earlier, but they stayed in touch by letter and similarly, Sarah was married with children and she got the occasional card or letter from her too. When she had moments of regret around relationships or marriage, she would blame Father Cullen, as, despite some fumbled attempts over the years, she didn't really enjoy sex, as it brought back painful memories of that fateful day in her kitchen.

She had also become slightly obsessive about cleanliness and hygiene, so her little apartment in the Gate Lodge was pristine at all times. Dust didn't get an opportunity to land before it was 'wet-mopped' or 'damp-dusted' away. She emptied and cleaned out all of her cupboards every week, wiping all the tins and packets with a damp cloth before returning them to the shelves and ensuring that everything was grouped correctly, and all labels were facing the front. Similarly, with clothing, she would sometimes change twice in a day if she felt she was sweating or if she dripped anything on her blouses or dresses. She would never simply wipe the stain, but she would strip completely and re-dress in a complete set of clean clothes.

Her wardrobes were immaculate with all garments also in colour and clothing groups, blouses, skirts, dresses, cardigans etc Although she could never accept it, she was hugely institutionalised after spending a lifetime in hospital. The staff were equally institutionalised, but they went home every evening, so were also accustomed to living in the wider community, but if anyone tried to change any routines or procedures, all hell would break loose amongst the staff and the threat of industrial action would be intimated.

Although Matron Jeffries had done a really good job as Matron, she never really rocked the boat too much, so staff were pretty used to getting their own way regarding major changes being implemented. Managers would often rather have a quiet life than go into battle constantly with staff who were resistant to change.

The one thing which she never spoke about, but which constantly caused her great pain, was the loss of her daughter at the hands of the Nuns and the daily guilt and shame which this created. How is she doing? Where does she live? Is she married? Does she have grandchildren? The shame which she brought on her family, prevented her from ever discussing how she felt about her child.

She didn't believe that she was entitled to feel anything, as, it was she who allowed her new-born baby to be taken away from her, even though she was only a child herself. She imagined what she would look like and what it would be like to meet her, but she never believed it would happen so she didn't dwell on such thoughts for very long. She felt that, maybe this was also the reason why she couldn't give herself to anyone, as she felt unworthy of their love therefore couldn't give them hers.

The hospital routine and her compulsive behaviours were the only things in her life which she felt an element of control over, even though it wasn't really control, it was just a set of rituals and routines which made her feel safe, but, except for the early time with Sister Jeffries which was very traumatic, she had always felt safe within the hospital walls. The bulk of her pain had occurred, long before she ever came to this place.

The following year was Mabel's 50th Birthday and Matron laid on a big party for her on the Thursday evening, with a live band who played music by *The Beatles* and *The Shadows* and she enjoyed the modern ways of dancing which young people were now doing all the time. She still liked the old-style dancing as well, but she did like to let herself go a little with the modern pop songs. There were lots of fun dances as well like the Hokey-Cokey, when everyone joined-in and had a great laugh in the process. Just below the stage was a table where Mabel's 50th Birthday presents were displayed after they had been opened.

She had never seen so many presents before and was delighted with every single gift, but especially with the beautiful watch which Marjorie had bought her. She also got some perfume and earrings and some LP records, one of which was her favourite singer, Tom Jones.

Later in the evening the band stopped playing and all the lights went out as Marjorie came in with a huge cake with 50 candles, which Mabel had to blow out after everyone sang Happy Birthday. It was another of those beautiful memories which she had treasured over the years. She always tried to look on the bright side, even when everything seemed dark, and this usually helped things to be easier to manage. Once again, she lay in her bed, in her apartment, and felt huge gratitude for the love and support which she had in her life.

On the day following the party, she got up, as usual, and after having some toast and a boiled egg for breakfast (She liked boiled eggs because they didn't get the saucepan dirty!) she headed over to Matron's office to see what the day held for her. When she arrived, she was surprised that Matron wasn't in yet, but she thought she may be resting after quite a late night, so she got started on the cleaning and polishing. It was around 10.30 when Dr Fotheringham arrived at the office.

"Good morning, doctor," said Mabel. "I'm afraid that Matron isn't in yet."

"I know, Mabel, that's why I popped over to see you personally. I'm afraid I have some bad news for you."

"Oh no!" screamed Mabel. "Not Matron!"

"I'm afraid so, Mabel. Her husband said that after having such a lovely evening at your party, she went upstairs to bed, and when he went up, some twenty minutes or so later, she was lying on top of the bed, so it was very quick, which, in itself is a blessing as she didn't suffer. It will probably have been a heart-attack, but we will find out soon enough."

Mabel was devastated by the news as, despite their troubled beginnings, they had become like family and were very close. The doctor left as soon as he had delivered the news, so she was alone, looking around the office and wondering what was going to happen. She was suddenly filled with fear and dread about the future and about how she was going to move forward without her dear friend beside her. She sat at her desk and began sobbing uncontrollably at the loss of her friend, feeling despair for the first time in many years.

After a time, she locked up the office and slowly walked back to the gate-lodge apartment, where she sat alone and wept until she had no tears left.

It took a great deal of hard work and courage for Mabel to 'pull herself together' in order to attend the funeral, as she felt absolutely lost and heartbroken. After all they had worked through in order to become such close friends, she had been taken, just like everyone else. She was angry with God as it felt like yet another let down on his part. How could he allow this awful thing to happen to her when she had finally found such happiness? Her anger was seething quietly, just beneath the surface, as she left her apartment, dressed fully in black, for the funeral service, which was being held in the Hospital Church.

On the short walk through the grounds, she was stopped several times by staff and patients offering their condolences and support, which lifted her resolve slightly. Marjorie's family welcomed her at the church door and showed her to a front seat. "Oh, I was going to just sit back a few seats," she said to Marjorie's husband.

"Oh, no girl," he replied. "You are family, and you're sitting with us!" She was deeply touched by the kind gesture and sat down at the end of the front pew. The service was very sad, with beautiful hymns like *Abide with Me*, and as the coffin was being carried out at the end, Mabel was invited to join the family in walking behind, which she accepted willingly. As she slowly got towards the middle of the Church on the way out, she was overjoyed to see a very frail, but still very much alive, retired Matron, who had been her strength for many years.

Matron signalled that she would see her outside and, once Marjorie's coffin had been placed in the black Hearse and it slowly departed, Mabel anxiously looked around the gathered crowd, hoping to see Matron. She spotted her standing at the side of the main door, also dressed in black and relying heavily on a walking stick.

"Matron!" she called as she ran towards her and threw her arms around her.

"Steady, Mabel, you'll knock me over!" she said as she returned the huge hug.

"I'm so happy you could come, Matron," said Mabel, beginning to cry again as she truly loved this lady who had taken a chance on her, all those years ago. "I'm just feeling so lost." She cried.

"Mabel," said Matron, "the pain is very acute at the minute, because a large part of your life has gone. A major relationship is over, and you will feel lost for as long as it takes you to come to terms with it." And she held Mabel as she wept.

"I'm 80 years old now and have very few people left who grew up with me. As you know, I never married or had children, so when I go, that's it!"

"Oh, Matron," cried Mabel. "You'll always have me. I'll always be here for you."

"I really appreciate that, Mabel," said Matron as they started to walk. "There's some tea and a buffet in the Rec Hall," said Mabel.

"Oh lovely," said Matron. "I'm bloody famished!"

The breakfast was a more light-hearted affair than Mabel had imagined, as her family, like Marjorie, were full of fun and laughter, so they regaled the mourners with tales of her antics over the years and how her temper got her into trouble on many occasions, a fact which both Matron and Mabel were very aware of.

"But she changed, Matron, she really did," said Mabel.

"Seldom have I seen such rapid and long-term change in a person, Mabel, and she credited most of it to you my dear!" said Matron warmly.

"Thank you, Matron," said Mabel with a smile.

As the gathered family and friends started to meander out of the hall and back to their lives, most of them approached Mabel, not Matron, to thank her for coming and to give her their condolences on the loss of her friend. She was very moved that so many people saw her as part of the family and not simply a 'Mental Case' or a 'Looney' which she had been called many times by groups of kids, when they saw her leaving the hospital gates.

"You're very loved, Mabel Murphy, and you must never lose sight of that," said Matron. "I wish I had a fraction of the love and support you have in your life."

"You're right, Matron, and I sometimes forget that," said Mabel. "I need to remember that more often."

"Why don't you start popping over to see me on Sundays for a bit of lunch? The bus stops right outside the hospital and right outside my door. It would be lovely to see you," said Matron kindly.

"I would love that, Matron!" said Mabel. "And I can do any jobs you need doing."

"No, no, no," said Matron. "You're my friend and my guest, and I won't have you lifting a finger." This made Mabel feel very precious and happy. She felt her anger with God reduce slightly as he had re-connected her with Matron. They agreed that the weekly visits would start the following week and the retired Matron left for home, smiling in a taxi.

Back at her apartment, there was a large, sealed envelope waiting for her, with simply 'Mabel' written on the front. She placed it on her small coffee table and hung her coat up in the wardrobe before making herself a cup of tea and sitting down to see who had written to her. She carefully opened the brown envelope and, inside there was a smaller, sealed white envelope and a small package. She opened the white envelope and immediately recognised the handwriting as she unfolded a letter:

Dear Mabel,

If you are reading this, then I'm dead and buried. 'Pushing up daisies' as they say! I wrote this in February 1965, as I hadn't been feeling very well, after some tests, my Doc said I had a heart condition, I could have had surgeries, but I was never a great patient myself, and it was very risky, so I decided to just to roll the dice and see how things went without treatment. If I've lasted a year or more, I've done OK!

Firstly, I wanted you to know how ashamed I have always felt about the way I treated you when you first came into E2. It was unforgivable and it haunts me. I know you forgave me, but I never forgave myself. Maybe over on 'this side' I'll manage to get there eh? Let's hope so!

Secondly, I want to thank you for everything you have taught me over the years. You may not realise it but, until we met, I was heading to hell in a handcart. I was constantly angry and hated everyone and everything, but you managed to somehow break through and see the real me. It was a frightening moment when I knew you could 'see me' but it changed my whole life because, it let me see that maybe the real me wasn't that bad after all. You, and only you made this possible, and helped me to do the same with my family and other friends.

Years later, you then gave me the courage to believe in myself and to apply for the Matron's position. You believed I could get it before I did, and it was your belief in me that encouraged me to 'give it a bash' and look what happened! Some of the happiest years of my life have been absolutely down to you my dear friend.

I know you will be feeling very sad and lost at the minute, because I know you very well Mabel Murphy, but just know that I will still be watching over you and making sure you don't 'fuck things up' without me! (As if that could ever happen!)

I have tried to leave you a little legacy to make sure you will be OK and in the hope that you will truly forgive me for my past. You deserve so much more.

From the bottom of my failing heart, I love you, and I thank you, and I wish you everything you could ever wish for yourself.

Take good care my very special friend and saviour.

Marjorie xxx

PS. My family are your family, and if you ever need anything, you know where they live, so don't hesitate to go and ask. Xx

Mabel wept quietly for her special friend, and at the beautiful words which she had just read, and she vowed to treasure them always. She then opened the small package which contained something in gift paper. She carefully opened it to discover Marjorie's beautiful large, navy-blue enamel and silver badge from the School of Nursing, which she wore on her uniform every day. The back was engraved 'Marjorie Griffiths, Registered Nurse' and Mabel knew that receiving it was one of her proudest moments. She kissed the badge and placed it on the table, proud to have been given such a memento.

She opened the next item, which was flimsily wrapped in brown paper. There was a hand-written note, again in Marjorie's hand, which simply said, 'You deserve this for all your years of hard work. Marjorie xxx'. There, beneath the note, was a deposit book for the British Linen Bank. She had never seen one up close, so opened it and there was the statement, 'Marjorie Jeffries, in trust for Miss Mabel Murphy, to be made available on death'.

"Oh my God!" said Mabel, as she turned page after page and saw deposits going back for years and years. As she reached the last page, she saw a final deposit of £20.00, made about a month before, and an available balance of £540.00! She dropped the book with the shock and felt her heart, beat faster. She lifted the payment book up and looked at it again and again, before she could take in the enormity of the gesture.

She held the letter and gifts against her chest and gently rocked back and forth, whispering, "Thank you, Marjorie. Thank you."

13

It's 1971 and things are changing again, how Mabel hated change! Matron was still alive but now being looked after in a care-home, south of Croydon, so Mabel hadn't seen her for a few months as it was an awkward journey with multiple buses, and it made her anxious. There was a new Matron whom she already knew as Sister York from the D2 on the female block, but who was now called a Service Manager, which Mabel hated, but she happily kept Mabel in her role. Who better to guide or advise than someone who knew the hospital system inside out!

The NHS had expanded and some hospitals had closed down or merged, and some were given the title 'Special Hospitals' which housed patients who were dangerous to others due to psychotic or disordered behaviours. There were one or two challenging patients from Surrey Hills who had been transferred to Rampton as they were extremely difficult to manage in an open situation. There had also been some investment and new wards had been built, in the style of Villas rather than gigantic blocks, then the blocks themselves were refurbished and divided into smaller dormitories with only four to six beds in each.

As a result of this, they had built a small block of 6 x 1 bedroomed 'flatlets' for patients who were doing well in their rehabilitation and would be going back home at some point. Although technically still a patient, Mabel was given the largest apartment upstairs, and was the senior resident, therefore 'in-charge' of the unit, a position which she relished, but which she also took great pride in and performed very well indeed. She was becoming prone to occasional bouts of anxiety/confusion, but these seemed to alleviate when she had focus and responsibility. She often did better therapeutic work than the staff, as she knew the system inside-out and was able to say things which staff couldn't.

In the training flats, she had labelled all the cupboards and drawers and had little reminders for the residents on how certain things should be done and how to operate the washing machine or cooker. There was also a 'buzzer system' to her apartment, rather like the modern warden-controlled accommodation. This meant she did less hours with Matron which was a longer-term phasing-out plan so that she didn't have the trauma of suddenly not being needed, so she didn't start until 11.00 and she finished at 2.00. Miss York brought in hospital domestics to do the cleaning, in order to ease the workload, so Mabel mainly made drinks and did some admin. By now, it was really a specially created position which wasn't needed really as Sisters became ward managers and took on new challenges such as recruitment and budgetary management.

About 18 months later, after a severe chest infection and pneumonia, her very first Matron, Joyce Higgins, passed away peacefully in the care home. There was no funeral to speak of and Matron had asked that it should be very brief, with no eulogies, so that is what happened. The staff from the care home organised a short cremation but did not invite Mabel as Matron didn't want her to be upset, however, like Marjorie, she appeared to have left her something in her last will and testament.

It wasn't delivered in an envelope though, she had to meet with a solicitor no less, to discuss the legalities of the will. Miss York, the service manager gave her permission to meet in the committee room and when she arrived for the meeting, there sat Mr David Burke with several documents in front of him. Mabel acted very calmly as she was mourning her Matron, but the curiosity about what was happening was also killing her.

Once she was seated and everyone had a drink, he began to read, "This is the last will and testament of Miss Florence Biggins, of 25 Hawthorn Drive, Banstead, Surrey." He went on to list a whole lot of personal assets, jewellery, insurances and pensions, personal savings and investments, and her three bedroomed detached house in Banstead. The solicitor said that her total estate value was around two hundred thousand pounds! Mabel was impressed that she was able to have gathered so much wealth during her life and wondered what trinkets she would be receiving.

"I, therefore, bequeath my whole estate, minus taxes and legal fees, to Miss Mabel Murphy, for her dedication and friendship over a lifetime. She was the daughter I never had and gave me the joys that I missed by never becoming a mother. She is a worthy benefactor and I hope that my legacy will ensure that she never goes without, should our political masters decide that people with mental health issues are a burden and 'de-fund' the system. I wish her health and happiness." Signed just over one year ago.

"So, Miss Murphy," he said with a smile. "You are now quite a wealthy woman, and it would seem from what I understand, a well deserving one." Mabel was lost for words, stunned, shell-shocked, moving in slow-motion.

"What the hell just happened?" she said in disbelief. She had been in the house and it was beautifully decorated with lovely furniture, but she couldn't see herself in it. It was big and grand not really her style, she thought.

"Can we sell the house?"

"You can sell whatever you like, Miss Murphy."

"Mabel, please," she replied. "But I would advise you to take some time to understand exactly what you have. Don't think of selling anything at this point, think of how you can get the best return on your investment, and we can advise you on that."

"OK, whatever you say," she replied.

"No, not that either, Miss Murphy," said Mr Burke, "you must begin thinking strategically, studying and understanding what you have and making decisions which will benefit you. We are always at your service for advice and guidance."

"Thank you, Mr Burke, I have a lot to think about," said Mabel as she shook his hand.

"Oh, Miss Murphy," he called as she was leaving. "Don't forget this." And he handed her a wooden box.

"What's this?" asked Mabel, it's the jewellery and the various deeds and policies mentioned in the will.

"Thank you," said Mabel as she carried her precious cargo back to her apartment.

She sat down on her sofa and opened the box to see the most beautiful pieces of jewellery, some of which she had seen Matron wearing over the years, but some which she had never seen. She lifted up a gold locket and chain with a small diamond embedded on the front. As she opened it, there was a photo of Matron on the left and on the right, a photo of a handsome young man in a World War I uniform. On the back was inscribed 'David Seaton. 1898–1917 Always Loved'. Mabel broke down in tears at the realisation that Matron had lost her one love in the great war. This is the reason why she never married and had children, she still loved David Seaton. How tragic, she thought as she continued to go through her treasure trove.

She met with Miss York later that day and told her of her good fortune. "Oh, Mabel," she said, "you're a very lucky lady, but you so deserve this!"

"Thank you, Sister York, sorry, I mean, Miss York, I can't get used to this modern stuff! To me, you're Matron!"

Miss York laughed and said, "I feel the same, Mabel, this new and modern language takes time to get used to."

As they sat down for a cup of tea, Mabel took a deep breath and said, "Can I ask for your help with something, Miss York?"

"Of course, you can, Mabel, how can I help?" she replied.

"Well, it's a bit embarrassing, but you know that before I was admitted here way back in 1931, I had a baby which was taken by the nuns and adopted?"

"I didn't know the detail, Mabel, but I knew that, at some point you had given birth before coming here."

"Yes, the nuns were very cruel and didn't let me keep the baby at all, she was adopted very quickly, and that was that."

Miss York nodded her head and listened intently. "What I'm trying to say is, although I haven't openly spoken about it much over the years, she has been in my thoughts every day, and the older I get, the more difficult the feelings become. I was wondering if there is anything I can do to find out how she is and if she's happy?"

"Oh Mabel, how awful this must be for you, but as the law currently stands, once a child is adopted, there is no way to easily trace them and there are laws about birth parents not being allowed to contact them, mainly for the protection of the child," said Miss York.

"I thought as much," said Mabel. "So even with all my money, I cannot find her."

"I'm afraid not, Mabel, but I will certainly check and make sure that what I am saying is correct."

"Thank you," said Mabel, wiping her eyes with a tissue.

"There is something else I wanted to talk with you about Mabel, just to keep you in the loop," said Miss York. "There is a new movement growing within government and the NHS regarding the advantages and disadvantages of large mental hospitals such as Surrey Hills. There is some talk of closing them down, not for a long time, but they do not see the benefits of keeping lots of people locked up, who could be living outside."

"Well, that's ridiculous!" said Mabel angrily. "What about all those poor people who came here because they couldn't cope outside, or because outside didn't want them!"

"I agree that many of our patients would struggle to be outside, but people like yourself, who are intelligent and were only sent here for having babies? For goodness' sake, Mabel, that can't be fair," said Miss York.

"It may not be fair, but it's done and it's too late to turn the clocks back, Miss York. I've been here since I was a teenager and it's all I know. This is my family, my friends and my job and there ain't no one throwing me out!" said Mabel defiantly, with her familiar anger still just below the surface.

"I know, Mabel, but I just wanted to let you know that it is being discussed in government. I will keep you up to date with any decisions."

During the summer of 1974, Mabel decided that, for the first time in her life, she wanted to go on holiday. She spoke to Miss York about it and, as she was terrified of flying, she decided that she wanted to spend a week at the seaside, somewhere on the South Coast. Miss York was very supportive and even suggested that she should also go with her, just for a little support should she have any anxious or confused episodes. This made Mabel happy, and they agreed on The Promenade Hotel in Eastbourne, which looked quite grand in the brochure photos. Seven nights, bed, breakfast and evening meal with entertainment in evenings and a day's trip to Brighton midweek.

They arrived safely on the Saturday and were shown to their rooms, each of them had a single bed, dressing table and wardrobe, with their own en-suite bathroom, which Mabel had never seen. She unpacked her suitcase and hung up all of her new outfits in the wardrobe and carefully arranged her other clothing and underwear into the dressing table drawers. Her room had a bay window looking out to the sea and she was thrilled as she sat in the small armchair looking out. There was also a children's train which ran up and down the promenade and she could see donkey rides on the beach and what looked like a puppet show. Mabel and Miss York met downstairs for afternoon tea in the 'Seaview Room' and were served tea with a selection of beautiful sandwiches, scones and cakes.

"Isn't this lovely, Miss York?" said Mabel. "Please, Margaret," she replied.

"Yes, it is beautiful indeed, Mabel."

After tea, they took a walk out of the hotel and down to the beach, which was a mixture of shingle and sandy stretches closer to the water. Mabel breathed in the sea air and felt wonderful. She looked at Margaret and said, "You know? I'll be sixty very soon, and this is the first time I've been to the sea, or stood on a beach, or seen a donkey outside of a photo. I feel like a little girl on her first holiday!"

"That's lovely, Mabel, enjoy every moment and new experience," said Margaret.

"Do you want a donkey ride?"

"Yes, please, if I'm not too big." And very soon she was being led along the sand on 'Hercules' the donkey who had no trouble carrying her slender frame. As she dismounted, she couldn't stop laughing with joy and excitement.

"I can't believe I just did that!" She laughed. "What's next?"

"Shall we take a walk on the pier?" said Margaret. "Perfect!" said Mabel and they headed back up to the promenade and onto the Pier which was very busy and full of activities. At the entrance, there were a variety of ice-cream stands, fish and chips stands, and gift shops selling rock and very saucy postcards. Mabel was quite embarrassed as she picked one up before realising there was naked ladies on the front, and she screamed and out it back! The long boardwalk was lined with benches where you could sit in the sun and, every so often there would be a funny wooden painted character which had a hole cut out for your face and a photographer took a picture. Mabel and Margaret had a photo taken with Mabel as a fat lady in a swimsuit and Margaret as a mermaid swimming past. They laughed so much their sides were aching.

At the end of the pier was a theatre and a penny arcade which had lots of slot machines and other amusements where you could win prizes. They both sat at a prize-bingo stand and Mabel won a set of three tea-towels with images of Eastbourne on them.

"Well done!" said Margaret as they began to head back to the promenade.

"This has been one of the best days of my life," said Mabel.

"Aw, Mabel, I'm so glad you're enjoying your holiday," replied Margaret, "and there's plenty more to come." The rest of the week was filled with new experiences, even Mabel's first swim in the sea. They saw different bands and magicians every night in the hotel and the trip to Brighton was one of Mabel's favourite days. She actually said, out loud, that she wouldn't mind living there, which made Margaret very happy, the very fact that Mabel was thinking of other possibilities for herself.

When they returned, the hospital seemed very dull and drab in its appearance and the atmosphere felt really down and heavy compared the constant fun and entertainment in Eastbourne. "I never thought I would ever say this, but I'm not ready to come back here yet, I could have done with another week," said Mabel.

"You can do whatever you want," said Margaret. "You don't have to stay here you know."

"I think that's what I mean, Margaret. I've never contemplated not being here, because for most of my time, I wasn't allowed to leave. I know I've had the choice to leave for quite a while, but I was frightened. The last week has taught me that I don't need to be frightened, I could probably be OK if I left," said Mabel anxiously.

"Just thinking out loud Margaret, you're not getting rid of me that easily!" Mabel spent the rest of the day going around the wards with sticks of rock and seaside gifts she had bought for lots of friends, regaling them with funny stories about her week at the sea.

14

It's 1985 and, once again there have been many changes in Mabel's life. She is still living in the top flat in the training block, but she is almost 70 and is no longer working in the old Matron's office. Margaret York was promoted to a regional position and was replaced by a male nurse, Michael Swinton, who was now the Service-Manager, and, after lengthy discussions, Mabel felt that she would be more comfortable working with a female, so she did a few hours every day with the medical secretaries in the doctors' offices. She only made drinks and tidied around, but she loved being with the three women who worked there, and it kept her connected to what was going on. She liked Michael Swinton, but she just felt uncomfortable being manged by a male and spending so much time alone with him.

'Care in the Community' had started to become a reality in some areas and some of the wards and departments had already closed down naturally as they had stopped any new admissions. The doctors were now also holding clinics in community-based facilities and Community Psychiatric Nurses (CPN's) had taken the role of maintaining patients in their homes or in supported living premises. Mabel had met with some of the newer, more progressive staff who were full of ideas for her, but she often felt that they didn't quite understand her story and why she didn't want to move out to a block of flats where she didn't know anyone. She regularly got into arguments during what was called 'Reprovision of services' meetings, when highly paid staff would present what she felt were, ridiculous plans and which she knew would never work, so, in no uncertain terms, she told them so.

Her input was actually crucial in the formation of 'friendship groups' which helped to ensure that, even when people were being moved out, they had some say in who they wanted to live with and in who they didn't want to live with. An extensive piece of work was carried out so that people who wanted to stay together could do so, and this entailed a lot of negotiating as most patients had come from London Boroughs who would have to pay for the continuing care after closure.

The staff also had to come to terms with the huge changes approaching, and the reprovision meetings would often descend into heated arguments over minor details such as plans for patients becoming known as clients. An elderly Irish ward sister stood up and said loudly, "I am a registered nurse therefore I work with patients! Prostitutes have clients therefore I will have no part of it!"

The place descended into uproar at this rather hysterical argument, but it showed the strength of feeling against the major changes which were inevitably approaching. Mabel was invited to a meeting with the reprovision officer, a lady called Anne Cruikshank, where she was given a list of choices including several shared accommodation options with other clients or a bedsit in a low-level council block. "I'm not living with a load of other people and staff wanting to bath me! That's terrible after all my years in this place. And a bedsit?

How am I supposed to manage out there with lots of young kids calling me names and all sorts of things. You go and live in a fucking bedsit!" she said angrily as she blessed herself for swearing.

"We don't want to upset you," said Anne. "We're only trying to do the best for you. Do you have any friends who you would like to live with?"

"No! I bloody well don't! They were all members of staff and they're all dead!" she screamed, before breaking down in tears.

"Why do you have to do this? It's terrible!"

"There is one more option, Mabel," said Anne, "your bank account is quite healthy, so you could buy yourself a place that you liked?"

Mabel turned red in an instant. "And how the fuck do you know what I have in my bank account?" she screamed and blessed herself again.

"Well, it's a matter of record, Mabel," replied Anne. "And is your bank balance a matter of record? How much do you have saved?" snapped Mabel furiously.

"How dare you tell me how much money I have and what I can and can't afford! Who do you think you are coming in here, fresh from some college or university and telling me my own business? No! Fuck off and leave me alone!"

Anne turned scarlet and began to gather her papers and put them back in her brief case. "I'm sorry," she tried to say but Mabel had lost all of her tolerance.

"No! Not another word you pompous cow! Fuck off!" and Anne quickly left the room with her tail between her legs.

Mabel took a deep breath and smiled to herself. "Still got it," she whispered quietly.

Over the next few months Mabel was taken to see many places, but always found a 'get out clause' which meant she couldn't take it, usually because it was in a council estate and she was frightened of young children. Eventually, and at the end of the road with ideas, the reprovision team asked the CPN (Community Psychiatric Nurse) team if they could help so they arranged a meeting for an assessment with a new Scottish CPN called Michael Keating.

They met in one of the new offices with bright new chairs and tables and huge windows out to the beautiful grounds. Michael made them both a drink and very casually sat down opposite. "So, Mabel," he said with a smile. "What do *you* want from this?"

Mabel was shocked, as it was the very first time she had been asked this question in such an open-ended way. Every question she was previously asked only gave her a yes or a no answer as it was do you like this or do you like that. Now she could actually think about what she wanted. She liked this new CPN, he was different and warm in his manner.

"To be honest, Mike, I would like a small place somewhere close to here so that I can still come in and see everyone."

"OK," said Mike. "We can look at that. But you will be restricted by budget if you choose this option via the current budgets and plans."

"I have my own funds, Mike, so I can do it myself, and then I will leave the building for the hospital when I die."

"That's very generous," said Mike. "But let's find a house before you give it away to someone else, eh?"

Mabel laughed out loud and became all bashful. "You're terrible!" she said. "You know what I mean."

"I'm only joking, of course I know. What sort of house are you thinking of, Mabel, detached, semi-detached, apartment?" he asked.

"Two bedroom semi-detached, in a nice street with no horrid kids," she replied confidently.

"Great! I can work with that, Mabel! I'll pop down to the estate agent and get some brochures for you to have a look and, if you like any, we can go see them."

"Oh, thank you, Mike," she said, feeling like a schoolgirl with a crush.

"No problem, Mabel, I'll catch up with you this afternoon, in fact, why don't you come to my office at 4.00 pm. It's the large Portakabin just by the car park."

"Thank you, Mike, I'll see you then!" said Mabel with a wave.

At 4.00 pm, Mike made two coffees and they sat down to look at houses. "They're very expensive in this area, Mabel, but there's a few which may suit you," he said. "Oh how. Exciting," said Mabel. "Let's see them then."

As each one was handed to her, she would make comments such as 'Maybe' or 'Garden too big' or 'too far away' but Mike was aware of her compulsive traits and had saved the best till last.

"And there's this," he said as he handed her the details of a newly built, link-detached house, only a short walk from the front gate, in fact it was built on land which was sold off by the hospital.

"Oh my!" said Mabel. "This is absolutely beautiful!"

"It is, Mabel," said Mike, "shall I make an appointment to view?"

"Oh, yes please," said Mabel with a beaming smile.

Two days later Mabel and Mike walked into the leafy drive approaching the Surrey Meadows Estate where they were viewing number 9, Larch Avenue which was surrounded by mature trees which had previously been part of the hospital grounds.

"Oh, I remember this when it had the old mortuary on it!" said Mabel.

"Don't say that too loud," said the estate agent.

"Nobody will buy it." And he laughed.

"I'm more afraid of the living than the dead," said Mabel.

"Me too," said Mike as they walked up the path to the front door. Everything was brand-new and pristine, which Mike knew Mabel would love.

"It comes fully carpeted throughout with all white good supplied," said the estate agent.

"What's white goods?" whispered Mabel.

"Fridge, washing machine etc."

"Oh, I'm getting them free?" asked Mabel.

"Well, they're included in the price, so you're actually paying for them," said Mike. "But it saves you from having to go out and buy them."

As they were shown around the compact home, all that could be heard from Mabel in every room was, "Oh, it's beautiful." As they came to the end of the tour, she said to the estate agent, "I'll take it," which made him and Mike laugh.

"What are you laughing at?" she said giggling.

"You sounded like you were buying a quarter of barley sugars," said Mike and Mabel went into hysterics laughing.

"You're terrible, Mike, you're always taking the mickey!" Mike explained to the agent that it would be a cash sale and helped Mabel to fill out and sign the required paperwork. The agent gave them details of how to pay by a counter cheque etc and hoped that the handover could be completed within the next two weeks.

Mabel was more excited than she had felt for years, and the following week Mike took her to one of the newer superstores where she could choose new furniture which the hospital said they would fund as she had bought her own accommodation, so Mike had arranged for everything to be invoiced directly to supplies manager at the hospital.

Every time she saw something she liked, she would say "Oh but Mike, it's very expensive" to which he replied, "You bought a house Mabel, you're winning financially, buy it!" and she would laugh. She even chose a double bed, after spending her whole life in a single bed.

"Go on, girl!" shouted Mike. "You might meet someone who wants to move in!" which threw Mabel into hysterics.

"Mike! Stop it! You're making me blush," she said.

"Away you go, Mabel!" said Mike. "A blowtorch wouldn't make you blush! which sent her spiralling with roars of laughter."

She looked at the salesman and said, "I'm sorry about him, he's a patient in the hospital and I can't take him anywhere!" which sent Mike into gales of laughter. Eventually they had furnished the whole house and Mike said, "Is that you done? Anything else?"

"I couldn't ask for anything else Mike. I have everything," she said with such humility that it brought a tear to Mike's eye.

During her formal one-to-one sessions with Mike, they were exploring how she really felt about leaving, in order to make sure she was getting all the support required on her own.

She explained that for years, the thought terrified her, and she had to keep putting it out of her mind, but that since he had arrived, she had a different outlook and, although still frightened, she now felt that it would be OK.

She had her very own, brand-new place and was close enough to walk in and out of the hospital as she pleased so she felt that she couldn't have come up with a better compromise. "I only now have one concern," said Mike, "and it's a minor one."

"Go on," said Mabel.

"Well, at some point in the future, not yet sure when, but the hospital will be emptied and it will inevitably be pulled down." He saw the colour drain from Mabel's face and, as he approached to offer support, she put her hand up in silence, to stop him.

After she gathered herself, she said, "If I live long enough, I will deal with that terrifying event when it comes, but in the meantime, I prefer not to dwell on such scary thoughts."

"Well done," said Mike. "That's a good attitude and has served you well. Stick with that for the time being, then, if and when things change, we can make an action plan."

Over the next few weeks everything came together. She got her keys to the house, she had some little bits of decorating done and had all of her furniture delivered and placed in the right rooms, blinds and curtains hung, bedlinens stored, and bed made up, kitchen stores and equipment put in cupboards and drawers, and then she was all set to move in. There was an impromptu party held in the hall where she said her goodbyes as a patient, but she knew she would still be going in and out for a while to come. It felt very strange the day that she walked out of the main gates and knew that she would never stay there again. She was genuinely sad and frightened as she walked along the road towards her new estate.

Even though she was only a stones-throw away, she was anxious that she was on the wrong side of the wall. When she got to her front door, Mike was there waiting with a little gift bag. “Housewarming present!” he said as she opened the door and let him in.

“Aw, thank you,” she said as she opened the bag. “It’s a vase!” said Mike.

“It was about the only bloody thing you didn’t buy the other week!” he said. She laughed loudly and said, “You’re terrible, Mike.” And slapped him on the arm playfully.

“Listen, Mabel,” said Mike. “You’ve done an amazing job getting here and I just want to wish you every success. You’ve got my number if you need anything in between but I’ll see you every week for our sessions anyway.”

“Thanks, Mike,” she said. “I couldn’t have done it without you.” And she gave him a hug.

“Oh God, I’m honoured.” He laughed. “A hug from Mabel Murphy.”

“Think yourself lucky!” she said before erupting with laughter. “Oh, you’re terrible, Mike.”

15

As the '80s progress and Mabel is now a citizen rather than a patient, the country seems to change rapidly into a more selfish, self-centred culture. People start talking about everything in terms of cost and the Conservative Government begin to privatise the NHS by out-sourcing non-clinical services such as domestics and maintenance services. Surrey Hills Hospital is all but empty, with only a few wards still operating for adults with more complex needs, but much of the administration services for the whole NHS trust have moved into the premises until their new development of office-suites is completed.

The CPN team are still in the grounds but Mike Keating is very busy with the resettlement plan and Mabel has been doing well and quite independent for some time now. She still popped into the doctor's offices every day for a little while and then she would get a little shopping on her way home and cook for herself. It was one day when Mabel didn't show up for work that the medical secretary called Mike and let him know. "She's never done this before, so we thought we'd better let you know," she said.

"No worries," said Mike. "I'll pop in and see her." He left the office with a spare key she had given for safe keeping and walked around to her house. He knocked a few times and couldn't hear anything, then he heard the chain being unclipped and the key turning in the lock. As the door slowly opened, there stood Mabel in her housecoat, looking very unwell.

"Oh, Mike, come in. I've been up all night," she said, and Mike walked through the hall and into the kitchen and sat down.

"Do you want me to make a cup of tea?" he said.

"Oh yes, please, but don't make a mess!" she yelped.

"That's ma girl, straight for the jugular!" he quipped. "Haven't seen you for months and the first thing you do is have a go at me."

She forced a smile and said, "Sorry, I just feel awful."

"Have you eaten anything?" he asked.

"Not since yesterday," she replied.

"OK, let me make you a bite to eat," he said. "If you get back into bed and rest, I'll cook you something and bring it through on a tray for you. How does that sound?"

"It sounds good so long as you don't make a mess!" came her sharp reply as she headed back to her bedroom.

Mike hadn't been in her house for a while and was surprised at the extent to which her OCD had progressed in such a short time. Each cupboard was perfect and almost looked untouched. Her fridge and freezer only had fresh milk and almost everything else was 'boil in the bag' style meals, so he took a cod in butter sauce and popped it into a saucepan and heated a tin of peas, and some Cadburys Smash for her.

He also noticed that she had covered every single piece of carpet with the clear plastic protector which is really meant for the high-traffic areas such as the front hallway, so there was not a single piece of carpet visible in the whole house. Mike was concerned at Mabel's mental state and wondered if a short spell back in hospital would be beneficial for her.

She sat up in bed as he knocked on her door and called, "Lunch is served, madam!" which made her smile.

He laid the tray in front of her and she said, "I hope you haven't made a mess in that kitchen!" with a half-smile. He was happy to see her begin eating the food and, after he tidied the kitchen, he returned and sat on the bottom of her bed.

"Are you alright, girl?" he asked. "I've noticed that you've gone a little overboard with your cleaning and wondered if there was something else going on."

"I just don't like dirt," she said. "So I eat boil in the bag to save my pans, they're very nice you know!"

"The meals or your pans?" joked Mike. "What about the carpet protectors, Mabel? I keep expecting to see Torville and Dean doing Bolero out there!"

Mabel almost choked with laughter at that line and said, "It's not that bad! You're terrible, Mike!"

He looked at her and said, "It's an outer sign, that maybe something is going on inside, Mabel. Does that make sense?"

Mabel finished eating and put her cutlery down. Tears started streaming from her eyes and she said, "I just can't stop thinking about my baby, Mike. It's there all day, every day and I don't know how to stop it," she said.

Mike moved her tray and sat on the edge of the bed, holding her hand. "OK, Mabel, this is new to me, we've never discussed this before," he said quietly.

"I was too ashamed to tell you, I only ever told Matron, but there was nothing could be done, so I was left with it." She sobbed.

"Oh, Mabel," he said. "Let me look into it, some of the laws around adoption have been changed and, I'm not promising anything, but I'll see how the land lies and I will let you know as soon as I know anything. I promise."

Mabel continued to weep but was also laughing. "Thank you, Mike, I know I drive you nuts, but I know I can trust you," she said. "Whatever you can find out would make me very happy."

"If I do this for you, you have to promise me one thing?" he asked.

"Anything at all," she replied.

"Promise me that you'll stop eating boil-in-the bag and Smash!" Which made her laugh out loud again. "That's my girl." He laughed. "You look much younger when you smile!"

"Cheek!" She giggled.

The following day, Mabel was back in the office, bright and early and was welcomed by the other ladies. "Oh, we missed you yesterday!" said Brenda, the office manager. "We were so worried about you when you didn't appear."

"Oh, thank you, everyone, I was just feeling a bit under the weather, but I'm a lot better today," she assured them. It was around lunchtime when Mike popped in to see her.

"You got a couple of minutes?" he asked.

"Yes, of course. You want a coffee?" she replied.

"Yeah, go on then!" he said.

"Sit down, they're all at lunch," she said, so they both sat down at the empty desks with giant electric typewriters on them.

"I've been doing a bit of digging for you and, it seems the legislation has changed slightly, and children can trace their birth parents without any problems. Birth parents can also get some information via a legally appointed intermediary, usually a social worker. I've enquired about how to best do that, but the main concern that they have is the unreliable records which were kept by nuns and other non-statutory adoption agencies back in the day. It seems that, in some cases, they were little more than baby farms, and they made considerable profits from the misery of their enslaved women. Well, I'm sure I don't have to convince you of that one Mabel, but the social worker I know is going to see what records they kept at your convent home."

"Oh, Mike! Thank you so much! I know it's not a lot of information, but it's given me a little bit of hope. You're an angel!"

"Ooh, I doubt many people would agree with that, Mabel." He laughed.

"Well, you're my angel!" she assured him.

Her mood lifted considerably after that little piece of news from Mike, so she decided to go visiting the remaining wards and have a chat to the nurses she knew. There weren't many left on site as most had gone to the re-provided services in the community, however there were a few who were close to retirement who just couldn't manage the change and stayed on in the remaining wards, which was quite a lonely existence compared to the busy and vibrant hospital of the past. Mabel also felt very sad when she saw the closed off areas and broken windows in the old blocks.

She was an outspoken supporter of the old mental hospital system and often described the mass closures as tragic. "I knew hundreds, probably thousands of people who had a great life in hospital. It may not have been what some people considered a nice life, but compared to where many of them came from, and compared to how many of them were treated by the society outside, it was a safe place and they knew, even when their mental health was poor and they were psychotic or stripping off their clothes in public, they were going to be looked after and protected, not arrested and imprisoned. They weren't bad, they were ill, and although there were some bad staff and, at times, some awful things happened to some patients, including me, the majority of staff were very committed and hard-working, and most of the patients had a bloody better life inside than they did outside!"

As she knocked on the ward doors or rung the doorbells, she would get a wave through the glass strip in the door and a nurse would come and let her in. She always got a warm welcome and a cup of tea as the staff could spear her for information and any gossip which was floating around, and she loved imparting her knowledge to others! F2 had one large main room, divided by a chimney breast so one side was dayroom and other side was dining room. Straight ahead through the doors were sectioned off bedrooms, formerly large dormitories.

In the corner of the dayroom was a glass fronted office or 'Nurses Station' as some staff still called it. There were tall, sash windows along both walls which only opened a few inches for safety reasons and there was a kitchen with a fridge and hob and milk machine, but food was still prepared and brought to the remaining wards from the main kitchen in the large silver trolleys with folding top-lids and a drop-down door on the front which was another hot cupboard for metal trays. She sat at the fireplace with her tea, looking around the room and remembering all of the changes she had seen. From 40 bedded dorms, to 30 beds then 20 beds divided between 5 partitioned bedrooms. She felt a part of the very fabric of the buildings, like her energy had been absorbed into the system and that she had to be close to it in order to survive. She knew well that this was called 'Institutionalisation' but she didn't care. It was her life and her existence, and she believed that the people who were writing all the fancy reports had never experienced any sort of life which gave them the right to pass judgement on hers. Mother Superior was the first person she ever felt so strongly about, so much so that she beat her half to death all those years ago, but she never forgot why she did it and throughout the years, she did not allow anyone to treat her badly, well at least, not without a fight.

A few days later Mike saw her in the grounds and waved her over. She crossed the lawned area to where he was sitting and said, "Well, what you want?"

"I have a little news for you," he said suspiciously. "About the mother and baby home."

"Oh, yes?" she asked.

"It seems that they had a bit of a rather suspicious fire, not long after you had been there, so they are saying that some, but not all, of the records were destroyed. It's just a regular convent now, the whole mother and baby thing was closed down by 1950 and they just pray now, probably for forgiveness for all their sins."

"They weren't all bad, Mike, some of them were very nice but were afraid of the senior nuns who could be very angry and cruel."

"I heard a whisper that you had a bit of a battle when you went toe to toe with the boss lady," said Mike. "And that you were a bit handy with a baseball bat." He laughed.

"It was a heavy poker actually, and I saw red! I just couldn't stop myself!" she said.

"I'm going to try and get an appointment for you to go and see them with me, to find out what info they have about your child's adoption," said Mike

"Oh, that sounds scary," said Mabel, "but it needs to be done."

About a month later, they arrived through the gates of the Sisters of Mercy Convent, and Mabel could feel everything come flooding back. She began to shake and cry, and Mike had to sit in the car with her for quite a time, talking her down and reassuring her, just to get her breathing back under control. When she felt calm enough, she said "Right, let's do this!" and got out of the car. "I'm not a scared young girl anymore, so let's show these Nuns who I am," as she walked up the few steps and rang the doorbell. There were a few seconds before the door was opened by a young Nun, who simply said "Mabel Murphy?"

"Yes, that's me Sister, and this is my friend Mike," said Mabel.

"Welcome, both of you, please come in," she said as she ushered them into the all too familiar hallway from Mabel's distant past.

The smell was still the same, the highly polished wood mixed with freshly cut flowers which were always displayed by the large "Our Lady" statue at the foot of the beautiful staircase. She could feel her body trying to scream out and release her pain, but she focused on her breathing and stayed very calm.

"I'm Sister Constance and I haven't been here very long, but I will make you some drinks and you will meet Mother Superior very soon," Said the nun.

They were shown into the visitors' room which Mabel remembered as the doctor's office.

"You ok Mabel?" asked Mike.

"Better than I thought I would," said Mabel "Thank you for being here Mike, I couldn't have even walked through that gate without you."

"No worries," he said, finally seeing the damage that trauma had done to such a young and innocent girl.

The door opened and an older Nun slowly walked into the room and said, "I am the Mother Superior, but you can call me Sister Agnes. I actually remember you Mabel, I was a young Novice when you were here."

"Oh My God!" said Mabel, "I remember you too! You helped me when I was going into labour!"

"Oh, you do remember!" said Agnes, grabbing hold of Mabel's hand. "On behalf of the Sisters, I would like to apologise for anything you suffered whilst you were here and ask your forgiveness."

"Thank you, Sister Agnes," said Mabel with a warm smile
"Is that it?" said Mike, "Have you any idea what this woman has had to endure and still endures because of what happened in this building?"

"Mike!" said Mabel, "I would imagine that the older. Nasty ones are all dead now, so there is nothing I can do, and the novices were not much older than me when I was here, so I cannot blame them!"

"Thank you, Mabel" said Agnes "And I understand your anger Mike, I have spent many years repenting for my part in not reporting things sooner, I have also been very troubled by the history of this Order," she said.

"I'm sorry," said Mike, "I just find it difficult to accept the abusive way things used to be and the consequences of those terrible times. How many people are in the same situation as Mabel up and down this country. It's a scandal!"

"So Mabel," said Sister Agnes, "About your Daughter. As you may have been told, not long after you left there was a small fire in the records department."

"That seems to have conveniently happened in several convent homes Sister," said Mike defiantly.

"I don't know anything about anywhere else, only here," she replied.

"Sorry again Mabel" said Mike.

"My own memory tells me that your daughter was adopted by a young couple who lived somewhere in Sussex, possibly Eastbourne or Brighton way?"

Mabel immediately broke down and said "Oh my God, maybe that's why I was drawn to that area. I've stayed in Eastbourne for holidays several times over the years. My God, I may have bumped into her or even met her without knowing!"

"I'm sure their name was Dickens or Dixon or something similar," said Sister Agnes. "I seem to remember them writing to you for a while Mabel?"

"Yes Sister, but Mother Superior made sure I never got the letters. The lady also promised she would make her middle name Elizabeth, after my Mum," said Mabel.

"I'm sorry we couldn't be of more help Mabel, and I'm so sorry you've had to suffer so much over the years. As you say, they're all either dead now or there are one or two being nursed in care homes. You are not the first of the girls to come back and you won't be the last, but I have tried to be as open and honest as I can with every single one. It is a terrible tragedy and I ask God's forgiveness on a daily basis."

"Thank you, Sister," said Mabel as she stood up to leave. Mike looked ashen and angry, "It seems to me that they all got away with it," he said, "Scot free! Every last one of the cruel bastards!" and he put his arm around Mabel's shoulder and left the room, once again into the stunning, ornate hallway. "Sisters of Mercy, Sisters of the poor, Sisters of whoever, and look at the opulent surroundings! All of it funded by human slavery, cruelty, and misery. I think every one of you should be in prison!" he said as he led Mabel down the outside steps. "Please Mike," she said "Enough! Goodbye Sister Agnes and thank you."

"Goodbye Mabel, and if you need to come back for any reason, please let me know."

As they sat back in the car, Mike put his head on the steering wheel and began to cry.

"Mike, whatever's wrong?" she asked.

"I don't know how you've survived all this shit Mabel. You're a better person than me, 'cos I would have fucking killed them all!" he said.

"That's why I ran away Mike, because I started hurting people. I almost killed the Mother Superior when I attacked her. It was terrible, and if I had been made to go back there, I would have killed her and a good few of the others," said Mabel "The hospital saved me from myself Mike, that's why I'm so grateful."

"You're one amazing lady Mabel," said Mike. "Very special."

On the way back to the hospital, they stopped at a pub and had an early evening meal where Mabel also had a sweet sherry "Oh Mike," she said, "I feel a bit tipsy."

"Just keep your hands to yourself," he said jokingly, "I don't want to crash the car!"

Mabel threw her head back and let out an enormous guffaw "Oh you're terrible Mike!" she said through breathless laughter.

16

Its 1990 and Mabel is celebrating her 74th Birthday with a few old friends in the remaining medical offices at the half-demolished hospital. The wards have finally all closed, and the relocation of patients completed. The remaining healthcare staff were given early retirement and the small block of offices which remain, are due to be moving out within a few months when the final phase of the new Headquarters is completed. The land has already been sold for a huge amount of money and a substantial housing estate will be built on the old site, some of it "affordable," but a large part will be a "de-luxe, gated-village."

"I bet you could tell a few stories about this place!" said Brenda, drinking a small glass of white wine.

"I could write a book!" said Mabel "But they probably couldn't publish it!" She laughed.

"It's a sad day in many ways," said Margaret, one of the newer secretaries "I feel like I just got to understand the old hospital and now it's gone."

"You missed the best years" said Mabel, "This place used to be thriving and alive with people. 1200 patients and hundreds of staff. It was like a small town all on its own," she went on, "and it operated like clockwork, kitchens, laundries, domestics, nurses, auxiliaries and patients. Everyone knew their jobs and how important it was to work together. If one department stopped working, it affected every other department, so people worked together really well."

Brenda, who had been there for a number of years said "Oh, yes. When I came here, it was a bustling place, full of life. I met my husband here; he was a van driver. And the social club was the best venue for miles, we had some fantastic nights over there. Yeah it's very sad, but I guess that's progress."

"So they say," said Mabel, "but I bump into ex-patients when I'm out and about, and none of them seem too happy in my opinion. They're sitting staring at four walls a lot of the time, whereas here they had so many people to talk to and mix with. I'll never agree that it was a good thing, but maybe that's just me."

"Do you ever stop moaning Murphy?" Laughed Mike as he arrived late from a meeting.

"Oh, shut up you!" said Mabel laughing, "He's terrible," she said to the gathered crowd.

"Yes, but you love me, don't you Mabel?" asked Mike as he poured himself a drink. "I've got something for you Mabel" he said, as he handed her an official looking brown envelope. "It's from the social worker I know," he added. Mabel took the envelope and gently opened it, revealing official-looking paper with Surrey Hills Social Services Dept Letterhead.

Dear Ms Murphy

Following some investigation regarding your child's adoption from the Sisters of Mercy Mother and Baby Home, Kent in 1931, we can confirm that the official paperwork has been destroyed by fire, but that the current convent residents have been very helpful in our investigations and we are confident that we may now be able to make formal contact with someone whom we believe to be related to the adoptive family in question.

Unfortunately, I cannot give you any further details at this point, and any future progress is dependent on what they may wish to do with the information given to them. As you are aware, you do not have any legal right to contact them unless they agree for that to happen, but please be assured that my team are doing all in their power to make this possible.

Yours Sincerely,

Christine Brown, Approved Social Worker,
Families and Adoption Services

Mabel read the letter in silence and began to cry. Mike put his arm around her and said, "Nearly there Mabel, whatever happens, you'll know all you need to know, so it's all good."

The gathered friends looked slightly puzzled to see Mabel upset, but she stood in the middle of the group and said "I'm not upset, I'm relieved. None of you know this, but the reason I ended up here way back in the 1930s, was because I had a baby. It wasn't acceptable like it is nowadays, and it brought shame on my family, so I was sent to a bleedin' mother and baby home, and my beautiful little girl was adopted. I never really told a soul about it when I got here and I felt ashamed ever since, but Mike has done an amazing job of helping me to find out anything I can about her. This letter seems to be saying that they think they know where she may be, but they're not allowed to tell me, unless she gives permission."

The secretaries were all very emotional at the honesty of Mabel and took turns to give her a hug and tell her how special she was to them.

"Get yourself a small sherry," said Mike "I think this deserves a toast! To Baby Murphy. Here's hoping she finds her way home!"

The group responded by raising their glasses and saying "Baby Murphy!"

Through her tears Mabel said, "Well she ain't no baby now, she'll be 60 and probably a grandmother!" She put her arm around Mike's waist and said "I couldn't have done any of this without this man's help. He's a cheeky bugger, but I do love him!" and everyone began to laugh.

"Let's just keep, our fingers crossed, eh?" said Mike with a warm smile.

About one week later, Mabel had popped into a new supermarket which had opened nearby in anticipation of the new and expanding housing estate. She was pushing her trolley and was slowly looking at all the new products which she had never seen before, as she usually found supermarkets a bit too busy and tended to use a small "mini-market" near her house. She was looking at some toiletries when she suddenly felt an excruciating chest pain, causing her to fall forward on to her trolley clutching her chest. She couldn't draw a breath inward, and the pain started to go down her left arm, causing her to let go of the trolley and fall to the ground.

"Can someone call an ambulance please!" called a member of staff as she bent over Mabel. "I'm Julia and I'm a first-aider, can you tell me what is happening for you?"

Mabel struggled to talk but managed to say "chest."

"Is it also going down your arm?" asked Julia and she responded by nodding. "Ok, I'm just going to loosen your jacket and top buttons, just keep trying to take deep breaths for me and the ambulance should be here soon," said Julia reassuringly.

Within a few minutes, Mabel felt the pain start to ease off, but not disappear and then she heard the familiar sound of the siren approaching. Within minutes, she was inside the ambulance wearing an oxygen mask and wired up to an ECG machine. One paramedic was working with her as the ambulance headed back to the hospital. "Looks like you may have had a bit of a heart attack," he said, but we'll get you checked properly when we get to A+E.

Mabel felt very embarrassed as she was rushed through the swing doors and into a screened bay, where she was re-attached to a heart monitor and a nurse called Frances hooked her up to a drip and took some bloods which were sent to the lab.

"Oh, I'm so sorry to be so much trouble," said Mabel "Don't give it another thought," said Frances, "that's what we're here for."

They also took some details from her and were a bit surprised when she gave her next of kin as "Michael Keating, my Community Psychiatric Nurse."

"Ooh, that's a bit of a mouthful," said Frances.

"Oh, wait till you meet him, he's lovely!" said Mabel, now starting to feel much better.

"I have a feeling I have already met him Mabel, is he based at the old Surrey Hills?" said Frances

"Yes! That's him!" she replied "Can you call and let him know I'm here Frances? Thank you."

Mabel was now in her nostalgic element, being looked after by a load of nurses and doctors. "Oh, you're so kind" could be heard all over the department.

Mabel was moved to a medical ward and, by lunchtime the next day, most of the test results were back and she saw a very important-looking consultant doing his ward-round and gradually getting closer to her single room. She looked at herself in her bathroom mirror and made sure her hair was tidy, then she hopped back into bed just in time for the small knock on her open door.

"Miss Murphy? I'm Mr Williams, Consultant Cardiologist," he said with a broad smile

"Hello doctor," replied Mabel.

"How have you been since yesterday?" he asked.

"Well, I feel like a fraud for taking up a bed because I feel fine doctor," she replied.

"Well, let me tell you that you are not a fraud at all, it's good that you came in because all of our tests show that you actually have angina, which is a heart problem, but we can give you a couple of meds which will settle it down. One of them is a little spray which you use when you feel a pain coming and it eases it away. How does that sound?"

"Oh, that's wonderful doctor, thank you so much!" gushed Mabel, adoring the male attention.

"Nurse will sort you out with a prescription and you can get yourself off home, but if it happens again and the spray doesn't do the job, dial 999 and get yourself back here," said Mr Williams

"Oh Doctor, I can't thank you enough. You're an absolute saint!" said Mabel in the throes of a gratitude attack.

Soon afterwards, Mike arrived wearing a doctor's white coat, a female nurses hat, pushing a wheelchair and carrying a tartan blanket purely to embarrass Mabel.

"Get yourself in here old lady and I'll wheel you home!" he said as he stood outside her door.

"Oh! Go away, I'm not getting into that! I walked into this place and I'll walk out thank you very much!" she said smiling.

"I'm only joking love, I know there's nothing wrong with you, just needed a bit of attention from a handsome doctor!"

"Be quiet you! Someone might hear and think you're serious!" she said in a quiet but determined voice.

Mike took off the costume and put it in the chair. "Come on girl, let's be having you!" he said as he proffered his arm.

"Oh, thank you," she said as she linked arms and was escorted through the hospital to the car park. "You're terrible Mike!" she said as she laughed loudly.

She plopped down on her comfy sofa and Mike put the kettle on. "We need to have a chat Mabel" he said as he sat down opposite.

"What's that then?" she asked.

"Angina doesn't mean that you've gotten away with anything Mabel, it can be a warning to take it easy and slow down a bit," he said. "You're 74 years old and you're still going out to work and tramping all over the place. You never sit still!"

Mabel pulled herself up to a straight sitting position and suddenly looked very indignant. "Listen here to me Mr High and Mighty! Would you rather I just lay down on my bed and died? The reason I've reached 74 is exactly what you say, I have kept myself busy since I was a teenager, because my life was so shit that I couldn't bear to stop and look at it! Being busy and tramping all over the place is exactly what has kept me alive! When I had the attack in the shop, I thought I was going to die and, actually, I wasn't scared, I was OK with it. The last thing I need now is to suddenly become an old lady, just in case I have another attack!"

Mike sat quietly, then looked at Mabel and said "I'm so sorry Mabel, you're absolutely right, but can you just slow down a bit? Stop running?"

Mabel laughed. "You're never happier than when you're telling me off mister!"

"It's my life purpose Mabel!"

Mabel relaxed back into her seat and said "Oh shush!" as she picked up her tea and began to drink. Mike tidied up the house and cooked a little dinner for Mabel.

"Oh, I love ham, egg and chips," said Mabel. "Are you sure you don't want anything?"

"No, I'm fine love, I'm meeting up with some friends later so I'll eat then," he said "Are we friends again?" he asked.

"Of course we are, you silly thing. I've forgiven much worse than that! Remind me to tell you about Sister Jeffries one of these days."

Several weeks later, Mabel received another official looking brown envelope from Surrey Hills Social Services, hand delivered by Mike. Again, she carefully opened the sealed part and unfolded the letter:

Dear Miss Murphy,

Following our recent correspondence regarding your non-statutory adoption, via the Mother and Baby Home previously addressed in our discussions. I can now officially tell you that we have traced your daughter and we have made her aware that you would like to meet her. We have not yet had a response, but I am very hopeful that, at the very least, we may be able orchestrate a supervised meeting for thoughts and feelings on both sides to begin to be addressed.

I hope to be able to bring you some positive news very soon, but in the meantime, I wish you good health

Yours Sincerely,

Christine Brown, Approved Social Worker,
Families and Adoption Services

"Oh, Mike!" she screamed, "They've found her!" She sat down and began to shake with the news. Tears fell and she said "Oh, God. I can't believe they've found her!" "That's fantastic news Mabel!" said Mike as he put his arm around her shoulder. "I can't imagine how you must be feeling." Mabel's whole body seemed to release years of stress and tension and she leaned into Mike and sobbed quietly. "You're almost there," said Mike

17

Mike had noticed, over a number of months, that Mabel seemed to be getting a little more forgetful and at times confused, and despite what he had said to upset her, he felt that it may be because she had less purpose as she only had the medical secretaries' office left to visit, and they would soon be moving. He spoke to his manager first and then went to see Mabel at home.

"What are you after?" Mabel said with a smile as she opened the door

"Well there's a nice welcome! I come all this way to see you just to get insulted!" said Mike as Mabel let out a roar of laughter. "Get the kettle on!" he said as he sat on the couch.

A few minutes later Mabel came in with a tray of tea and biscuits, laid them on her coffee table and said "Right! What's going on?"

"Well!" said Mike "I've had an idea and I wanted to run it past you."

"Oh yes?" said Mabel "Let's be having it then?" "Ok," said Mike "You know the medical secretaries are moving soon?"

"Yes" she replied.

"My team are also moving, but we're going to be very close by, just at the health centre."

"Oh, yes, that's not too far, is it?" she said.

"That's the thing," said Mike, "We will have a few offices and a meeting room, and we need someone to help us see to visitors and do drinks etc, and who better than you Mabel?"

"Well, I never!" said Mabel, "A few weeks back you were telling me to stay at home and now you want me back to work?" but she couldn't keep a straight face and burst out laughing. "I would love to help!" she said. "God, you had me there for a minute Murphy!" said Mike

18

Although Mabel loved Mike and they got on very well, she didn't really know much about his life outside of work. He seemed to be single a lot of the time, and liked "partying" as he called it. If someone was opening a bottle in the hospital, he could hear it and would usually be invited as he was full of fun and mischief. He didn't keep appointments on Monday mornings and usually skipped off early on Fridays as his social calendar was very full. She had heard rumours in the hospital that he might be gay, but she didn't like to ask him. Not that she had any problem with it but rather she didn't want him to think she was being too personal, so she just avoided the subject. She looked at him that day and, although he was, as always, the centre of attention and keeping everyone entertained, he didn't look his usual self. His eyes weren't connecting with her in the usual way and his face looked very drawn. She had mentioned before that he had lost weight, but in trousers and a tee shirt you could see it. Mabel was a bit concerned for her friend but didn't know how to approach him with it.

As it transpired, despite being a little pissed, he insisted on walking Mabel home, so she invited him in for a cup of coffee and, as she sat the tray on the table, where he was sitting looking exhausted, she just said "What's going on Mike?"

"What do you mean, I'm fine," he said defensively.

"How long have we known each other?" she asked "Well, it's been a good, few years," he said, "but I don't know what you're getting at."

"Mike," she replied, "you've done so much for me, and I am forever grateful to you, but I know that there is something wrong with you and I feel like it is serious and you're shutting me out! Now, I don't give a shit about your professional boundaries, I care about my friend who is losing weight and looks frightened."

At that point, she saw the mask fall and he began to cry. He appeared so vulnerable in that moment, that she quickly sat next to him and put her arms around him tightly.

"you can tell me Mike, what on earth is it?"

"Well Mabel," he said, "I was actually diagnosed HIV positive three years ago. I'm a gay man and, as a nurse, was very careful, but it still got me. I've done well for the past few years, but my T cells are very bad and I may be moving into a full-blown AIDS diagnosis. I don't know how long I have, or if some of the new treatments will help, but I'm not holding my breath. I'm being realistic about my chances, and they are not good."

"Oh you poor thing," said Mabel. "I'm here for you every step of the way and I mean that!"

"Mabel, you're actually one of only a few people whom I know actually mean it, so thank you," and he kissed her cheek, "Who would have thought I'd be croaking before you Murphy?" he said with a laugh.

"You're terrible Mike!" she said with a gentle squeeze of his arm.

Mike had a couple of weeks off work to try and rebuild some strength, and he popped in to see Mabel a couple of times during his break, but he still looked very thin and drawn. Mabel felt that living with the constant fear must have been a factor in his battle against HIV/AIDS. She gave him a nice card about being able to depend on your friends and a little crucifix which she had since the mother and baby home. "You know I'm not religious after my experiences with the Church, but this crucifix always seemed to give me some strength when everything felt like it was too much."

"Thank you Mabel," he said, "my family have completely rejected me so you'll never know how much your gesture means to me."

"They've rejected you," said Mabel, "what the hell is that about Mike? How can they reject you when you need them so much?"

"It's the whole sexuality and AIDS stuff that is too shameful for them, they don't want anyone to know."

"Well, I think that's bleedin' disgusting!" cried Mabel, "How can they do that to their own child?"

"I've kinda got used to them not being there through my life Mabel. When I came out, they asked me to move away as they couldn't tolerate the thought of anyone finding out. My bags were packed in record time and they even paid for my flat rental until I got on my feet. I've barely had contact in 20yrs so I wasn't expecting a miracle when I told them I had HIV…but a hug would have been nice."

"Well bloody hell!" she called in anger, her eyes glistening with tears, "Well you've bloody well got me and, if there's one thing I'm good at, it's hugs!" and she sat down beside him and pulled him in towards her. "Don't you worry," she whispered as she patted his back and allowed him to sob. She decided at this point to keep an extra special eye on Mike as she knew he would struggle to ask for help.

It was Mabel's first day at the new Health Centre where the Community Mental Health Team had a suite of offices. She was introduced to the reception staff and some of the other teams who were now based there, and she was very excited to be part of this brand-new venture.

"Mike, the offices are just beautiful. I look forward to keeping them clean and tidy and looking after your visitors," she said.

Mike showed her to the main office which the Community Nurses shared and, there in the corner was a little table and chair, with tea and coffee, kettle etc "That's your desk Mabel," said Mike as he pulled out the chair

"Oh, my!" she replied, "I've even got my own desk!" "You're the boss Mabel!" said Mike with a huge smile. "You're terrible Mike, but thank you for asking me to work here," she said gratefully.

Just then, a middle-aged lady wearing a green uniform came into the office.

"Mabel, this is Mary who's the domestic here, Mary, this is Mabel," said Mike and they both shook hands, "Pleased to meet you," they both said at the same time and Mabel said, "I know you, don't I?"

"We've never met, but I used to work in the hospital as a cleaner many years ago and I remember you too," said Mary

"You were in F2 weren't you?" asked Mabel.

"Yes! You've a better memory than me!" She laughed. Mike smiled, as he knew that they would get on and that Mary would be another person to keep an eye on Mabel.

There had been no new information from the social worker for a few weeks, so Mabel was becoming slightly disheartened, however Mike had put a call in to Christine Brown to get an update, so he called Mabel over to his desk and she sat in the visitor's chair.

"I've just spoken to Christine and she says she is very sorry that she hasn't been in touch with news, but it seems they have moved home, and didn't get the letter which was sent, so she has re-sent it to the new address which she has been given. She asked me to give you her sincere apologies for not getting in touch sooner." "That's a relief," said Mabel "At least I know it's still happening. I don't mind if she doesn't want to see me. Well, it would really hurt me, but I would be ok. I just want to know that she's OK and I want her to know that I didn't get rid of her. I want her to know what happened."

"I have an idea," said Mike "Why don't you write her a letter with everything you want to say, I can help if you like, and we can give it to Christine to give to her?" "What a great idea Mike! Thank you!" she said.

A few days later and after several drafts, they both agreed on the following letter and that the attack by the priest should not be mentioned at this point.

My Dear Daughter,

I hope you are well and that your adoption was a very happy one. I just want you to know that I have thought about you and prayed for you every day since you left me. You were never unloved or rejected, you are a victim of the way things were at that time. I fell pregnant when I was just a girl and was banished to a Mother and Baby home which was run by an order of Nuns who were, at times, very cruel and harsh to the girls who were there. I did meet your adoptive parents when they chose you as their baby and I begged them to take care of you. They said they would and also said they would use Elizabeth as your middle name, as this was my Mother's name. Anyway, the day they came to take you was one of the most awful days I can remember, but I gained some solace in the hope that you would be loved and cared for, better than I could at that point.

As it turned out, I became very unhappy and ran away from the home after assaulting the Head Nun, who was particularly cruel, and I ended up in a state hospital being looked after. I now have my own house and live independently in Surrey, and as I get older, I find myself thinking about you more and more. It would be lovely if we could meet one day but I understand if you feel that this is not a good idea, for whatever reason.

Lots of love,
Mabel Murphy, your birth Mum xxx

Mike took the letter to Christine Brown, the intermediary, and asked if it would be possible to forward it and she agreed that it would be a nice gesture.

It was less than a week later when Mabel invited Mike over as she had received a reply via Christine. Mike arrived within a few minutes and Mabel made a cup of tea for them both. Her precious letter was sitting, unopened on the coffee table.

"You haven't opened it yet?" shrieked Mike

"Oh Mike, I'm far too scared in case it's bad news…I'm bleedin' terrified!"

She handed the unopened letter to Mike and said "you read it; I can't stop bleedin' shaking."

"Are you sure?" Mike said as he opened the envelope and began to read:

"My Dearest Mabel

Thank you so much for your lovely letter which has made me very happy. As you suggest, my name is Maureen Elizabeth Herbert and my parents told me I was adopted from as early as I can remember. They have both now passed away, Dad in '85 and Mum only last year and they were fantastic parents so you can feel happy that I've had a good life. I did often wonder why you had to give me away, but my mum always said it was very, very, sad and that you were only a child, so I have never felt any angry feelings towards you, but I have aften wondered where you were and what you were doing. I didn't want to get in touch in case you were settled down with a family and no-one knew about me. I hope you understand, if I had known you were alone, I would have contacted you a long time ago.

I am a widow, my husband Tom died of Pancreatic cancer five years ago, but have two grown up daughters, Margaret and Caroline and they each have two children, boys funnily enough, Tom (9) Peter (7) Gerald (8) and Mark (6) so you are a grandmother and a great grandmother! I spent most of my life working as a nurse and my ex-husband was a doctor, so we've never wanted for anything really. I find myself thinking about you a lot too as I get older, in fact I'm crying as I write this as I feel so guilty that you've been alone for all these years. I wish I had known, as I would have tried to help you in some way. I guess we can't change what has happened, we can only change things moving forward.

I would very much love to meet you in person very soon and then, introduce you to your new family. Let me know a good time for a visit and I will drive over to you from Sussex. I live near Eastbourne which is lovely if you've ever been over this way, and I look forward to hopefully meeting you very soon.

Sending lots of love to my birth Mum

Maureen Elizabeth xxx"

Mabel began to cry in a way which Mike had never seen. She was wailing and struggling to control her body, but Mike grabbed her and, through his tears said "Fuck's sake Mabel, you've done it!" but she couldn't speak, she simply allowed herself to weep.

After a time, she composed herself and took Mike's hand "You know, I could never have done this without you." She said, "You've put up with all of my bad tempers and moods, never knowing if this was going to happen or not, but you kept me positive and on-track. Thank you Mike. Thank you."

"Mabel!" he shouted, "I had just stopped crying and now you've started me all over again!" They sat together reading and re-reading the letter and smiling at each other.

"We'd better get writing a reply Mabes, or we may miss the moment," said Mike "Let's get the visit sorted!"

Ten days later, Mabel's house was shining, she had been to the hairdressers and had bought a new outfit, and she was sitting waiting at the window for her daughter's car to arrive. She had made a lunch of sandwiches and cakes and the tray and kettle were ready for her arrival. Mike sat on the couch, invited by Mabel for support but also instructed to go if everything was going well.

"No sign yet?" he asked.

"This could be her I think, Look Mike," said Mabel.

He got up and went to the window where he saw a black BMW slowly coming up the street, with the driver looking at house numbers.

"Yep! That's her!" he said nervously as the car pulled into Mabel's small drive.

Mabel let out a gasp when she got out of the car. "Oh Jesus, it could be me getting out of that car!" she said, "She is my double!"

"Oh my God," Mike replied, "two peas in a pod!"

There was a gentle knock at the door and Mabel answered nervously. Her daughter looked into her eyes and said "Well, I don't need to ask if you're Mabel, it's like looking in a mirror!" and they both began to cry as Mabel stepped out and they embraced, holding each other tightly.

"Oh, my baby," cried Mabel, "I'm so sorry I let you down, please forgive me."

"Oh God, don't even think that," she whispered through her tears, "your decision gave me a fantastic life and I'm sorry you've had to carry this for so long."

They stood for several minutes, locked in a hug, stopping only to look at each other, then return to the hug. Meanwhile there was a slight "cough" from Mike in the doorway.

"Oh, sorry Maureen, this is my friend Mike who has helped me to find you," said Mabel as she released her grip

"I'm so pleased to meet you Mike," she said as she hugged him "and thank you for everything you have done to make this possible. I only wish we could have met sooner."

"It's my pleasure," said Mike, "she's a very special lady and I hope you can have many happy years together."

They sat down together on the sofa, talking non-stop, and were very quickly very comfortable with each other. Mike made his excuses and said he had to leave, which left them together alone. Mabel began to recount the day she was taken but Maureen stopped her and said, "you don't have to recall all that painful stuff for me. I know you didn't want to let me go and I know my adoptive mum always felt guilty because she had a feeling the Nuns didn't treat the girls well, but she couldn't conceive naturally, and they desperately wanted a baby so she carried that guilt with her."

"There was nothing she could have done love, they were a powerful force and, until fairly recently, nobody believed the stories. Your mum was very kind to me and kept her word by calling you Elizabeth," said Mabel reassuringly. Maureen then opened her large shoulder bag and brought out albums of photos to show Mabel, who loved looking at anyone's photos, but all of these were of her new family and she still couldn't believe it. "I'm so lucky to have found you," she said.

"I'm the lucky one," replied Maureen. "I've had a wonderful Mother my whole life and, now that she's gone, God has given me another."

As the afternoon went into evening, Mabel asked Maureen if she would like something to eat.

"Why don't I take you out for dinner?" said Maureen "Somewhere nice that you'd like to go to."

"Oh, that would be lovely," said Mabel, "There's an Italian Restaurant in town which looks lovely, but I've never been, well, you don't go to places like that on your own do you."

"Let's go there then." Said Maureen.

"Lovely," said Mabel, "but it's going to be late for you to drive home, would you like to stay the night? I have a spare room all made up."

"To be honest, I was hoping you would say that. I brought an overnight bag just in case we got on well and I didn't want to leave you, and that's exactly how I feel." "Aw, me too," said Mabel, "It feels like we've known each other forever."

At 7.30 pm, they sat down at their table in "Trattoria Parmagianni" in the town centre, and were handed a leather-bound menu each.

"Ooh, this is very posh indeed," said Mabel laughing, "You'll have to translate for me, it looks like it's all in Italian!"

"It depends what you fancy," said Maureen, "It's in sections, pasta, or pizza or chicken or fish. What are you in the mood for?"

"Well, I like a bit of chicken," said Mabel.

"How about chicken Kiev?" asked Maureen, "it's breadcrumbed and has got garlic butter in the middle?"

"That sounds perfect!" said Mabel. "And just order whatever else you think Maureen, I'm not a fussy eater."

The meal was absolutely beautiful, and they shared a bottle of wine which helped them to further relax and chat.

"I haven't done so much jawing since I was a girl!" Laughed Mabel. "And I still can't believe I'm sitting having dinner with my daughter."

"I know," said Maureen "I feel very blessed this evening." "Here's to us!" said Mabel, slightly tipsily, as they clinked their glasses. Mabel shared some of her childhood events which had led to her eventually being sent to hospital, but she made the decision never to tell her how she had got pregnant. Maureen did ask about her father during the meal, but Mabel just said it was a mistake with a local boy and she hadn't seen him since.

As they strolled back home, arm-in-arm, under the glow of the street lights, Mabel was as happy as she had ever felt. "I'm as proud as a peacock to be walking beside you Maureen," she said, "My little girl, back in my life and all grown up."

Maureen squeezed her arm and said "How do you fancy coming home with me to meet your family tomorrow? You're going to love them!"

"Jesus!" shrieked Mabel, "My heart's going to burst out of my chest I'm so happy right now! I'd love to come! I haven't told you this but I've been to Eastbourne several times, it's one of my favourite places!"

"You're kidding me!" said Maureen "Where did you stay?"

"I stayed mostly at The Promenade Hotel on the sea-front," replied Mabel.

"Oh my God, we may have bumped into each other as I used to pop in there some evenings in the Summer with Tom after walking along the beach. It was lovely, but it's a bit run down now I'm afraid."

"Really?" said Mabel "That's a shame."

"Yes it's a sad consequence of foreign holidays, no-one wants to be beside the seaside anymore, well, not if it's cold and wet!"

"That's very sad," said Mabel, "I had some happy holidays there and got to know the staff quite well."

"I'll take you for a walk down there tomorrow if you like," said Maureen.

"Oh, I would love that!" replied Mabel enthusiastically.

Back at the house, the tea was quickly made and they both continued chatting, predominantly Maureen chatting and Mabel listening as she was aware of not wanting to give a bad impression of herself. She shared examples of her "importance" to Matron and Sister Jeffries and how the hospital depended on her for many years, but she avoided anything to do with bad language or anger. "I'm not saying I was an angel," she said at one point, "but most of the time I was a good girl, provided people were nice to me. I can't stand a bully, so I got myself into a few scrapes defending myself over the years!"

Maureen was laughing, imagining the image of this quiet, elderly lady, sticking up for herself. "That must be where I get it from then!" she said "Oh I was terrible when I was younger!"

"No!" said Mabel.

"Oh yes I was! I got brought home once by the police because I beat up a boy who was bullying my friend!" she added.

"No!" Laughed Mabel. "You must get it from me!"

This gave Mabel permission to tell some milder tales of the nuns and Sister Jeffries, but she kept the darker events close and didn't feel able to share them with her daughter. As they headed off to bed, Maureen gave Mabel an enormous hug and said "Night Mum" Fighting back her tears Mabel said "Night Darlin', I'm so glad you're here"

Mabel lay in her bed, with the warm glow of a streetlight breaking through her curtains and she felt a contented warmth wash over her body and an uncontrollable smile take over her face.

"Now everything is as it should be," she thought to herself. "It's taken a lifetime of pain to get here, but now it all feels worth it. Thank you, God," she said for the first time in years.

As suggested, Mabel went with Maureen and spent and few days became a couple of weeks meeting her family in Eastbourne, She seemed to fit in very quickly and naturally and had everyone roaring laughter with her anecdotes and quirky little habits. They spent days out, went for walks, meals, to the cinema and theatre and picnics on the beach.

"Oh I've had the time of my life!" said Mabel, "it's as if I've always been here."

"Everyone loves you Mum; they feel the same. Why don't you give up your place and come live with us?"

Mabel was visibly taken aback by that suggestion.

"Have I said something to upset you Mum?"

"No my darling. Far from it," said Mabel. "There's just one more thing I need to do before I can uproot Maureen."

"What's that?" asked Maureen.

"My friend Mike, the nurse you met, has got that damned AIDS. He's beginning to get very ill but all of his family rejected him, so he is all alone. He's been there for me for these last few years, so I want to be there for him"

"Oh how sad," said Maureen, "But it's a huge responsibility Mum, are you strong enough to manage so much?"

"I've got to be Maureen, otherwise I wouldn't be much of a friend, would I?"

Maureen squeezed her arm and said, "I'm right here with you. Anything you need, just ask and I'll sort it."

Mabel was dropped home by Maureen a few days later. "I'll call you later Mum so that you can let me know how you're doing with Mike," said Maureen as she kissed her goodbye

"Thank you Darling," said Mabel, "I'm gonna go and see him now, see how he is."

Mabel unpacked and then headed straight to the nurses office.

"Is Mike in?" she asked as she popped her head through the office door.

"Oh Mabel," said Patricia the office secretary, "I'm afraid he's off sick."

"Oh no!" said Mabel, "Is he at home?"

"I'm afraid not," replied Patricia tentatively, "He's been admitted to Mayday in Croydon, I don't know much more than that I'm afraid," she replied.

Mabel sat down and stared at the floor, not knowing what to do next.

"Let me see if I can find anything out for you," said Patricia, "make yourself a cuppa and I'll make a few calls for you."

"Oh thank you Pat, you are a good person," said Mabel.

Two hours later Mabel found herself standing in Mayday Hospital, Croydon, clutching a piece of paper with directions to get to the infection control area on 1st Floor. She eventually saw the infection control sign above two locked wooden doors with a sign which said "Please press bell and wait" which she did.

"Can I help you," said the large male nurse as he opened the locked door

"Eh, I'm looking for Mike, er Michael Keating, I was told he was here."

"And who are you?" he asked.

"Oh, I'm his friend Mabel," she replied nervously.

"I think you'd better come in love," he said, "I'm Rob and I'm a staff nurse here."

"Thank you so much," said Mabel.

He showed her into a little side-room with some chairs and a coffee table. "If you can wait here, I need to get some permissions before I can give you any information. I know Mike has no family but I just want to check that you are the name he mentioned."

He returned a couple of minutes later and said, "yeah, its OK to talk with you so I need to tell you a few things before you see him is that OK?"

"Oh yes, thank you Rob," said Mabel.

"Well, firstly, Mike is very ill Mabel, his condition has deteriorated rapidly, and his immune system is very compromised. You may get a bit of a shock when you see him as he has lost an awful lot of weight and has some lesions on his face and body. He's also got a form of pneumonia which is making it very difficult for him to breathe. You are the only person, outside of a couple of close friends, who he has given permission to be allowed in, they've gone back up north so you've made his guest list," he said, trying to invoke some humour into the situation.

They walked through a corridor and Rob said "This is the room here." He gently knocked the door and stuck his head in. "Mabel is here, you ready?" he asked, he then turned to her and said, "In you go love, if you need anything, come and get me."

As the door closed behind her she looked at the sight before her and it filled her with fear and anxiety. There was Mike, once handsome, barely an outline in the bed-sheets, skeletal, covered in sores. He was slightly sitting-up and his long skinny arms were resting on the top sheet.

"Hello trouble," he said quietly, managing to force a smile.

"Oh Mike," said Mabel "How on earth has this happened so quickly." She tried to hide her shock and sadness but it was not easy.

"Ah, it's got me proper Mabel," he slowly whispered, "don't be too upset. I'm OK, they've got most of the pain under control but I've got lesions in my mouth and throat so I can't really eat, and if I do I get the most horrendous diarrhoea, so It's not worth the bother. I don't have very long, but I'm not too bothered as I don't want to carry on like this."

"Oh my dear Mike, I'm so sorry," sobbed Mabel. "It should be me in there, I'm old, you're only a young man! What kind of world is this!"

"Listen Mabel," he said with a knowing smile "I may be young, but I packed a lot into this short life. I had some great fun and got to know some great people over the years. I drew the short straw when it comes to getting AIDS but there's nothing I can do about it now. It's done."

Mabel held his thin hand in hers. "What can I do to help?" she pleaded, "Tell me what to do."

"You're here Mabel, you're doing it," he said "Just be here…I don't want to die alone" and silent tears fell from his eyes.

"I won't leave your side Mike; You've been the best friend anyone could wish for," she said as she stared into his eyes. As he drifted into a sleep she went into the corridor and waved to Rob.

"How long is he going to be like this?" she asked as Rob approached, "Is he going to die?"

"Oh that's a difficult one I'm afraid," said Rob, "he could go tonight, or he could last another week. It's impossible to predict. He may be very ill, but his heart is very young and wants to keep beating, but my instinct says it won't be too long now."

Mabel let out a gasp and lost her balance, grabbing onto a chair for support.

"Breathe," said Rob as he stepped forward to support her, "It's a lot to take in all at once."

Mabel composed herself, "I would never have believed this could happen. He looked after me for years and now I'm the strong one. He looks like a withered old man lying there, how can that be?" she said angrily. "Can I stay with him?"

"Of course you can," said Rob, "we even have a folding bed if you want to stay the night."

"Thank you Rob, you're very kind," she replied.

"Leave it with me and I'll sort everything," he said as he headed to another part of the ward.

Time seemed to pass very quickly as Mabel sat holding Mike's hand, chatting to him and reading him bits of magazines and books she could find. His pain-relief was strong and made him drift off to sleep regularly, but only for short periods. He would open his eyes after a few minutes and say "what time is it" and Mabel would reply "bedtime" with a smile and squeeze his hand gently. She asked Rob for the payphone trolley which he brought and plugged-in, so she called Maureen and let her know she was ok.

Mike knew she was there and would remind her of things they had done together, like buying her house. "I've never known anyone buy so much fucking furniture in one go in all my life!" he said as he tried to laugh out loud, but his voice was weak and shaky.

"Cheeky bugger!" replied Mabel, "I just wanted to get it all at once to save going back and forth!" She laughed.

When it got to around 10.30 pm and the night nurses had been in to see him and give more medication, Mabel decided it would be sensible to try and get some sleep, so she kissed Mike goodnight and climbed into her folding bed which Rob had made up with a quilt and pillow. She lay in the darkness listening to the "beeps" from the machines which Mike was wired up to and noticing the blinking of different monitor lights. If she listened really hard, she could hear him breathing, very slow, shallow breaths. Every so often she couldn't hear him breathing, so would jump up out of the bed to check.

"I'm still here," he would say with a cheeky smirk.

"Oh, you're terrible," she would laugh, as if there was nothing wrong.

It was around 3.00 am that she was awakened by a voice, and it was a night nurse leaning over Mike's bed.

"What's going on?" asked Mabel through sleepy eyes

"I think he's going now if you want to be with him," said the nurse warmly

"Oh My God!" cried Mabel as she rushed out of her bed towards Mike, who was breathing in a rapid, shallow pattern.

Mabel grabbed his hand and said "It's alright my Darling, I'm here with you, don't worry, everything will be fine." She looked at the nurse for support as her tears began to flow and she felt him ebb away.

"He's gone," said the nurse and Mabel roared from her heart like she'd never roared. The Nurse came over and held her tight, "He's at peace now my love, look at him. Look at his face. No more suffering. What a great friend you must have been to be with him at this time."

"He was a great friend to me nurse." She cried, "You've no idea."

After all the emotion had died down, the nurses were clearing out his bedside locker and they found an envelope addressed to Mabel Murphy.

"Isn't that you?" asked one of the nurses

"Yes, it is," said Mabel in a puzzled tone. "He didn't tell me about any envelope."

She sat down on the chair and opened it:

Hey Murphy!

If you've got this, I'm hoping you made it to see me before I crossed the rainbow bridge. I wrote this while I was still able to put some thoughts together. I have made a living will and it is with the Chaplain who is going to contact my parents.

They didn't want anything to do with me when I was alive so I'm not too bothered about what they think, so I've put down everything I should have said to them years ago. Let's call it a parting-shot! Needless to say, you don't have to take care of a thing, it's all under control. The relevant people have your telephone number to let you know about funerals etc It's all organised and paid for, but I just didn't have a date when I wrote this. Haha!

You have been the most amazing, strong and trustworthy friend I could ever have asked for.

Thank you, thank you, for everything you brought into my life, you made the last few years worth living and you were there when no-one else was. That's what a friend is Mabel.

Now enjoy the rest of your life with your amazing family and don't worry about anything.

I love you so much

Mike xxx

Mabel kissed the paper and held it to her chest

"Something nice?" asked a nurse

"Beautiful," said Mabel "Just beautiful."

A few days later Mabel attended a small cremation service with her daughter and grandchildren. There were a few staff from the hospital and Health Centre, but no family whatsoever. Mabel leaned into Maureen and whispered "How can family be so cruel?"

“There will be consequences for them Mum, they will have to carry this, long after everyone else has forgotten.”

Within a few months, as she promised, Mabel sold her house in Surrey and moved into Maureen’s house. She had her own area within the house where she could stay if she needed privacy or peace and quiet when the house was full of visiting children although this was seldom necessary because she loved her new position within the family. She felt truly loved and appreciated by them all and treasured each and every day.

As they all sat in the garden one summers day, Mabel looked around at what she was now a part of. Family joking and laughing, children screaming and arguing over toys, dogs barking at the commotion, she looked at Maureen and said “It was worth it Maureen.”

“What do you mean Mum?” said Maureen.

“Everything I’ve had to go through in my whole life was worth it, ‘cos look at what I have now. I’ve got everything I ever wanted and I couldn’t be happier,” she said as “happy tears” began to roll down her face.